AN EVIL OFFERING

A DI SCOTT BAKER CRIME THRILLER

JAY NADAL

INKUBATOR
BOOKS

Published by Inkubator Books
www.inkubatorbooks.com

ISBN (eBook): 978-1-83756-094-3
ISBN (Paperback): 978-1-83756-095-0
ISBN (Hardcover): 978-1-83756-096-7

Previously published by the author as Sacrifice.

*"Wherever you are, death will find you.
The ancient ways are still alive."*

ZULU TRANSLATIONS

Amandla avela empilweni entsha
Power comes from new life

Kwangathi lo mnikelo uletha ingcebo nenhlanhla
May this offering bring wealth and luck

Ukuphila kwakho sekuphelile
Your life is over

PROLOGUE

"*mandla avela empilweni entsha,*" Xabi whispered, watching as the life of the young child in front of him passed from one world into another.

The sacred words had been passed down through generations of Xabi's family as old and treasured spoken heirlooms. A final blessing given to the gods that meant power comes from new life. Many in the Western world could not understand or accept his traditions. But for those who believed, Xabi carried magical and mystical powers that delivered wonders far beyond human comprehension.

The circle of yellow flames flickered and danced as they cast their haunting shadows on the walls. Their orange glow reflected in the whites of Xabi's eyes. He knelt, waiting for the throbbing in his temples to subside. A solitary bead of sweat traced a path down the side of his face, evidence of the effort it had taken to sever the head from the rest of the body.

One sharp, clean cut and then a sense of satisfaction followed, surging through him. His sacrifice's blood-curdling, deafening, and ear-splitting screams only made the spell more powerful. He cradled the beating heart in his hands, savouring the passing of energy from one being to another.

The man who had accompanied Xabi stared on, watching in fascination as a life drained away.

Xabi's mood matched the darkness of the night. His actions neither excited nor saddened him. Rituals had become an integral part of his life for as long as he could remember. His mind drifted back to a time as a young boy. He had squeezed through the small crowd of people gathered in his village to witness a special occasion.

Xabi had not been much taller than knee height, pushing through the masses of limbs, curious to get a peek. The soles of his feet were hot and hardened by the rough stones. He watched the mysterious man crouch and then stalk in a circle around a child not much older than Xabi. The man looked different to the others. His eyes were large, scary-looking and red, like the night sky before the sun set.

The hollering and high-pitched howls from those watching served to only incite and fuel the sacred man.

In one hand the man held the largest of knives; in the other a funny-looking object with a gruesome smile on its face. Later in life, Xabi had learnt the object had been a human skull.

The noise of those gathered frightened Xabi. The women's high-pitched screams hurt his ears, and he brought his tiny hands up to drown out the terrifying sounds. Had they all lost their minds?

His heart raced, threatening to explode from his chest, as the noise rising to a crescendo of noise reverberated and circled him. Xabi buried his head into the leg of one woman when the man swung his knife at the child's neck. The move silenced the crowd.

The circle of flickering candle flames brought Xabi back to the present. He waited until the final twitches of the body signalled the ending of a life. The gods would be happy with this offering.

He completed the last of his prayers as he worked on the rest of the body. The gods had been kind in finding the perfect offering for him. No one would dare to question him. In the eyes of his believers, Xabi's powers inspired complete reverential respect mixed with fear and wonder. He moved in the shadows and worked in the darkness of night.

Xabi cleaned his instruments and placed them back in his case. Like that of a surgeon, each knife had a specific purpose.

After wrapping the body in a blanket, Xabi then bound the package in plastic sheeting, finally securing it with brown parcel tape. The other body parts would be disposed of later.

Xabi turned to his companion. "Next time, it's your turn."

———

THE JOURNEY across town was quick in the dead of night. With few cars on the road and even fewer pedestrians, Xabi drove at speed through the back streets. He preferred darkness so he could move unnoticed. The night brought with it a shroud of fear for people. It was when the ghosts, the devil, the witches, and the spirits of those betrayed and hurt rose to seek retribution and pain.

Well, his followers and the politicians and government officials back home believed they did.

Xabi pulled up on the outskirts of town. The road served as a divide between the urbanised sprawl and the scrublands that surrounded the estate. He opened the passenger door and stepped out. For a moment, he paused and scanned his surroundings for any signs of life. But all he heard were the screams from feral cats, a dog barking, and the distant sound of a police siren as it raced to an emergency.

The chill of the night stung his lungs as he took a deep breath. He would never get used to the cold. It was much warmer in his homeland.

Xabi took another breath, and together with his companion, they lifted the package and crossed the road. Sharp brambles scratched at him as he burrowed into the dense undergrowth. The sharp incline of the small hill laboured his breathing. As the ground levelled off, the lactic acid burnt his thighs. He paused for a short moment to catch his breath and glance around to make sure that his arrival had gone undetected. The pair carried on to the second short hill, which offered a dense covering of tall bushes and trees.

In the inky black darkness, Xabi could only see the outline of shapes.

He backed his thin body into an impossible gap in the tall, dense bushes, careful not to snag the plastic sheeting on the branches. He continued to drag the package whilst his companion huffed and hauled his end. The tightness of the space left little room to manoeuvre as Xabi laid the package on the ground and pulled loose foliage over it.

Kneeling, he muttered a final prayer and bowed his head before leaving.

1

Scott's mind might have been in work mode, but his body clung to holiday mode as he made his way along the seafront.

Christ, it's only been forty-eight hours since we arrived home.

Getting up had been a struggle for hi and Cara. She had pushed him out of bed after Scott had pressed the snooze button on his phone for the third time.

"You'll be late," she'd said.

His reply of, "No shit," had earned him a thump on the back.

"I should have listened to Cara," he muttered as he crawled in traffic towards the roundabout near Palace Pier, which often came to a grinding halt during peak rush hour. It was for that reason that he preferred to arrive at work early to avoid the jams.

He listened to Coldplay on the radio and smiled as he thought back to their time in Spain. It had been too long since he'd been away. He and Cara had enjoyed having one-on-one time together. He thought about the fun they had shared and laughed. The image of Cara screaming when she'd spotted a humongous cockroach on their balcony had been one moment he'd remember for ever.

Scott missed the warm, soothing rays of the Spanish sun. Already, there was a noticeable change in the weather since his return. The sun didn't feel as warm on his face as before he'd left, the nights were getting darker earlier, and the wind had picked up, dragging grey, bulbous clouds across the seafront.

Scott sighed as his mind turned to work and what lay ahead. The job was intense, the hours long, the praise short, and support from the top was inadequate. He knew that by the end of the day, the holiday would be a distant memory.

THE SMELL of bacon hit Scott's nose as he walked into CID.

Some things never change.

He glanced around to see some of Sussex's finest filling their faces. A mixture of smiles and puffed-out cheeks greeted him. Mike, Raj, and Helen tried to swallow their mouthfuls, leaving Abby to speak on their behalf.

"Aw, guv, good to see you back." She frowned. "I thought you would be more tanned?"

Mike interrupted, a pathetic grin on his face. "The guv spent too much time indoors..."

"Trust you to drop the conversation to the lowest at the earliest opportunity," Scott replied.

A mixture of half-eaten bacon rolls, half a Madeira cake, an empty box of Mr Kipling's Victoria slices, chocolate croissants, and pain au chocolat littered the space between the desks, courtesy of Raj.

Abby smiled. "We missed you, guv."

"Well, I missed you too, Abby. As for the others, I'm not so sure," Scott quipped as he glanced over at the rest of the team, who wore expressions of feigned shock. "I brought you back a few treats. Although I'm not sure you need them, judging by that lot over there."

He placed three large jumbo-sized Toblerones, some Spanish boiled sweets, and Valor chocolate to make hot chocolate on a nearby table.

"There's always room for holiday treats, guv," Raj reassured him.

"Get back to work, you lazy sods, and someone clear up the mess," Scott remarked as he strode off towards his office. Abby rose and followed him.

It felt good to be back. He was lucky to be surrounded by a good team, and they enjoyed having a laugh.

"Have I missed much?" Scott asked Abby as he fired up his PC. He settled into the seat of his well-worn chair with a puff of his cheeks. Abby sat down in one of the spare chairs on the other side of the desk.

"Nothing major, guv. Besides, I want to know more about the holiday." Excitement tinged her voice, and Scott knew she was desperate to get all the gossip.

He waved away the question, saying, "As I said, Miss Nosey Parker, what did I miss?"

Abby scowled and crossed her arms like a disgruntled child. "We are still following up on some minor cases, still making all the usual inquiries. Our main caseload has been following up on two homophobic attacks near some of the gay pubs in town, near the Bulldog and the Marlborough."

"Any developments?"

"Not much, guv. Some grainy CCTV images. We have one attack on film, but we've not had much joy in identifying the attackers. I'll grab the case file and all the other files too. We can go over them when you have a free moment?"

Scott stared at his screen and groaned when he saw his inbox. "That might be much later. I have three hundred and sixteen emails in my inbox in just ten days. Email overload, and half of these emails are crap."

Abby raised a brow. "Welcome back. Anyway, tell me about your holiday, *or*...I'll just get all the juicy gossip from Cara."

Scott imagined the conversation when Cara and Abby next met. They were like two old grannies at a bingo night. Lots of oohs and aahs. He thought it wiser to give Abby a quick rundown of his holiday, hoping it would get her off his back.

"It was lovely. Great food, lovely weather, and perfect company."

Abby's eyes widened. She held her hands out. "Is that it? Is that all you can say after ten days away? Mr Enthusiastic you're not." She patted down her jacket. "Where's my phone?"

"Okay, okay," Scott said, raising a hand in surrender. "We stayed in a lovely apartment. A Spanish urbanisation just twenty-five minutes from Malaga airport. It was a nice quiet place with no tourists, which was a blessing. We drove through Torremolinos and Fuengirola, and they were concrete jungles catering for the mass tourist market. The place we stayed in had Spanish residents and a few expats from the UK and Europe who had retired out there, so very peaceful and relaxing."

Scott pulled up a photo album on his phone and handed the phone to Abby for her to flick through.

He continued, "I could get used to it out there. It's such a relaxed pace of life. The funny thing was that on a Friday night we would be ready for bed around nine. Sea air, good food, out all day in the sun – you get the picture." When Abby pulled a face, Scott smiled. "Anyway, about that time of the night, the Spaniards would be firing up their barbecues for big family meals. You'd get this waft of cooked meats just drifting across the neighbourhood and in through our balcony window. You could see these small pockets of golden light in the darkness, from the barbecues scattered around us. Absolutely magical."

Abby closed her eyes a moment and smiled. "Hmm, sounds perfect."

"It was. I know where I'll be spending my retirement. And then about a five-minute drive down the road was a gorgeous little town called La Cala. We ate freshly caught fish in restaurants right on the beach – on the sand! I wish you could have seen it, Abby. It was such an amazing setting... And then one evening we went into the hills to a small town called Mijas Pueblo. We sat in a restaurant on a hillside overlooking the coast. Spectacular at night. The lights from the traffic and the neighbouring towns glittered in the darkness like jewels scattered over the land."

Abby sighed. "Sounds romantic."

Scott's mind drifted back to Restaurante La Alcazaba, where he'd held Cara's hand over dinner and gazed into her eyes. In that moment, everyone around them had melted into the background. The sound of Spanish guitar music and the clip-clop of horseshoes from tourist carts had echoed up from the town square beneath them. He'd caressed her hand as they'd savoured the closeness between them. Scott couldn't have been happier in that moment.

He cleared his throat, saying, "Moving along, how has the boss been?"

"Same as." Abby rolled her eyes. "Moaning, hovering, and giving us regular pep talks about what a great team we are."

Scott extracted himself from his chair and straightened his jacket. "I'd better pop in and see him before he sends out a search party for me."

He had another reason for seeing Meadows that couldn't wait any longer.

DETECTIVE SUPERINTENDENT MEADOWS waved Scott in and pointed his pen at a chair whilst rustling through a document and adding his signature to a few places. From Scott's position, he couldn't see what the paperwork related to. Whatever it was had Meadows nodding occasionally and curling his upper lip.

"First things first, how was your holiday?" Meadows asked without lifting his head.

"Fantastic, sir. I enjoyed it."

"Relaxed?" he asked as he fiddled with his tie.

"Yes, sir."

Meadows interlocked his fingers and rested his hands on the table. "Good to hear it. I've been keeping a close eye on your team whilst you've been away, and they've been doing a sterling job."

"Glad to hear it, sir. Any news on a replacement DCI?"

Meadows puckered his lips as if he had eaten a slice of lemon. "I wish I could say that I had some good news for you, Scott, but it comes down to a question of finances. As you know, we're spending over one million pounds on refurbishing the station. So it's a matter of costs versus refurbishment. We have to find the money from somewhere, and bearing in mind the constabulary needs to save over fifty million pounds over a four-year period, money is tight."

"I understand, sir. It's just that before I left, there was speculation we were still in the market to replace DCI Harvey."

"Things change quickly, Scott. The powers that be –" Meadows pointed to the ceiling, where the chief superintendent sat, one floor above "– and the CC are pushing hard to balance the books. The cuts come at the loss of over seven hundred officers and three hundred other staff. It's impacting everyone, and we all know morale in the lower ranks is taking a hit."

"So where does that leave us? Are we doing away with the rank at Brighton?"

Meadows shrugged his shoulders. "Your guess is as good as mine, Scott. We have a better chance of getting another DC for your team than a DCI, because it's cheaper."

Scott nodded and looked away. Any possible chance of him taking up an acting DCI role was slipping away.

Meadows leant back in his chair. "Listen, Scott, I know how you felt about DCI Harvey. That was then; this is now. We have a job to do, budget cuts or no budget cuts. We still do the best we can." He paused as he studied Scott. "Listen, I know we haven't seen eye to eye in the past, but we're on the same side and need to work together. Yes, you have a different managerial style. You're gung-ho, and perhaps I'm more ambitious than you, but between you and me, we can cover the DCI's responsibilities."

Scott was taken aback by the super's comments. He was about to defend his career aspirations when Meadows's internal phone rang. He raised a finger and answered it. The DSI remained impassive during the conversation, offering the occasional "hmm" before he replaced the handset.

Meadows pointed at Scott. "Your team is on. You need to head over to the Whitehawk – uniform have just taken a call. A dismembered body has been found by a local resident. It's the body of a child."

2

W ithin minutes of the call, the team had scrambled. Meadows's last words were, "Keep me informed as soon as you have control on the ground."

The journey to the Whitehawk estate took the team less than ten minutes. A heady mix of nerves, excitement, and sadness overshadowed the journey.

The team never looked forward to being called out to a body. They never knew what to expect. Serious injuries, differing stages of decomposition, and the circumstances surrounding a corpse's condition often made for uncomfortable viewing. That the early reports suggested a young child only added to the tension and concern.

Scott received regular updates over the radio as Abby weaved in and out of the streets of the estate. Different scenarios turned over in his mind. Was this an abduction and murder? Were there anxious parents waiting for news of their missing child? Or had this been an act of violence by a parent?

The two cars were waved through the outer cordon that

had been set up some distance away from the crime scene. Curious residents looked on at the comings and goings of every police vehicle. Many waited in small, silent huddles, while others gathered and conducted whispered conversations.

Scott, Mike, and Abby signed in with the scene guard and donned their paper suits, overshoes, gloves, and face masks. Scott instructed Raj and Helen to speak with the first responders and to organise door-to-door enquiries. He then sent Mike and Abby up the hillside towards a white forensic tent that had been erected on the inclined bank.

Scott took a moment to survey the scene. From where he stood, the outer edge of the housing estate sat to his left, and the grassy bank to his right. He couldn't see evidence of CCTV on any of the surrounding houses. Without the presence of any shops either, the chances of getting video evidence appeared slim.

Despite the large police presence, a distinct stillness and calmness set the tone of the scene. Officers had the innate ability to switch into work mode regardless of the heinous nature of the crimes they attended. More than half a dozen police cars were parked in a row. A black private ambulance signalled the presence of the mortuary assistants. Two white scientific services vans confirmed the attendance of Matt Allan, the crime scene manager, and his forensic teams, and Cara's silver Ford Focus sat at the back of the line.

Scott picked his way up the two small, steep inclines towards the white tent. Several SOCOs were combing an area twenty yards around the tent, accompanied by half a dozen police officers in blue overalls and blue, police-issue baseball caps. He watched them pause as they marked a trail of trodden grass, identifying the direction in which the perp had entered the area. The dry, firm ground made for sharp, brittle grass. Very little rain over the summer had left the ground parched.

Abby stood outside the tent, staring at the ground, her arms wrapped around her. She glanced up as Scott approached. He observed her ashen face and red eyes with concern.

She shook her head. "It's grim, guv."

Scott pursed his lips. "What do we have?"

"A child, male, black. Wrapped in a blanket and plastic sheeting." Abby paused as she took a few deep lungfuls of air. "He's missing his arms and head."

Scott took a moment to take in Abby's words. Part of him wanted to believe he'd misheard, but she didn't negate the grim revelations. He *had* heard right and needed to see for himself.

He lifted the flap and entered the tent. A large evergreen bush had been cut back to reveal a small clearing in the middle. Large arc lights lit the scene. Cara, as pathologist, was jotting down notes. Brilliant white flashes of light from the SOCO's camera blinded Scott.

He stared down at the small naked body that rested on a red blanket, which sat on top of blue plastic sheeting. Without the head and arms, the body looked more like a disassembled doll than a child.

Words failed him; he sucked in a breath to keep his composure. Even if he saw a dead body every day for the rest of his career, he'd never get used to seeing brutally murdered kids.

He needed to focus, but his mind kept repeating, *What kind of monster does this to a child?*

Scott knelt to inspect the remains. He prayed that the child had not suffered what was clearly a violent death. He glanced over at Cara, who had paused from her writing to stare at the corpse.

Away in her own thoughts, she muttered, "Nice welcome back, hey?"

"Don't you wish we had never come back?" He sighed. "Time of death?"

"The body is cold and stiff, so rigor is still present. I would say within the last eight to thirty-six hours max. However, bear in mind there is no evidence of decomposition. I would suggest that time of death was within the last eight to twelve hours. Had the body been warm and stiff, then I would have said three to eight hours. But we also have to take into consideration the external temperature. It wasn't cold last night, and the body-temperature drop was slowed by being wrapped in a blanket and plastic sheeting."

"What else can you tell us?"

Cara let out a huge sigh. "No more than six or seven years old, and no less than five, I'd guess. There's a tear in both shoulders, not clean amputations, as you can see. From first inspections, it looks like the head was severed with a clean cut as opposed to sawn. But I'll know more when I get the poor boy back. There's significant blood loss on the blanket, so that would suggest that the injuries were sustained whilst the victim was alive. Left leg, dislocated. The chest cavity was opened not long after his other limbs and the head was removed."

"A frenzied attack?"

"I'm not sure. I don't think he put up much of a fight. There are no defensive marks or lacerations to the rest of his body. Perhaps there were on his arms, but..."

Scott nodded and gave Cara a reassuring squeeze on her arm. "I'll see you outside in a bit."

He walked away from the tent to gather his thoughts and to control his emotions. A mixture of deep sadness and anger stiffened his body. Anything to do with children struck a chord with him. In his eyes, killing a child was the worst act of violence that could be committed.

"I told you it wasn't pretty." Abby sniffed as she came alongside him.

Scott coughed and cleared his throat to refocus. "It doesn't get much worse than that. Whoever did this is one sick, twisted individual. They found the arms or head?" He nodded at the officers combing the ground.

"Not yet. They could be anywhere around here or even dumped in another part of town," Abby replied, scoping the terrain.

"Who found the body?"

"It was an old fella taking his dog for a walk. The dog darted into the bushes. A little Yorkie. Despite calling it back, the dog wouldn't come out. Poor old sod had to crawl in there on his hands and knees. That's when he found Dave tearing through the plastic sheeting."

"Dave?"

"His dog." Abby shrugged. "Uniform have taken a statement from him. Raj is going to speak to him as well. The gentleman needed medical attention for the shock."

Cara appeared at the entrance to the tent. She joined Scott and Abby as Matt Allan wandered over. They huddled in a circle to discuss their initial findings and the next steps.

"I think it makes sense to widen the search area for any further evidence and the missing body parts," Scott said.

"That will be a big job," Matt replied. "We are talking about a strip of land more than half a mile long and a third of a mile wide."

"Well, an aerial search won't reveal much. We are not going to pick up any heat sources. But the dogs can pick up a blood trail. Abby, can you organise that for us?"

Abby nodded.

"When can we get the PM done, Cara?" Scott asked.

Cara blew out her cheeks. "I can do the PM for tomorrow. I have too much on today, first day back and all that."

"I know you're busy, but we need some answers on this quickly," Scott pleaded. "It's a child. It's someone's son and even brother?"

Cara checked her phone. "Okay, okay. We'll get the mortuary team to take the body now, and I'll conduct the PM later on this afternoon. I'll put in a call to the Sussex police and get another pathologist over to help with my workload today. How's that?"

Scott nodded in appreciation just as Mike joined them. Mike had followed the bank up to the top of the hill and then tracked along the ridge to identify anything else of interest. On his way back down, he had ventured into the tent and then came out moments later, looking unfazed.

"Two hundred yards over the ridge is the outer edge of Brighton racecourse. So I can't imagine that the body was brought from there," Mike said, thumbing at where he had just come from. "So it looks as if the road at the bottom of the hill is the likely entry route for whoever dumped the body here."

Matt agreed, saying, "The trail of compressed grass we've identified appears to come from the road. There's only one track going there and back. We searched the road in the immediate vicinity of the track, and there's nothing of interest. There are no blood traces, fabric, tyre tracks, or anything. Our only hope for evidence is from the blanket and the plastic sheeting, plus anything else that we can lift from the body."

Scott gave his final thoughts. "Well, if the current search reveals nothing, then perhaps we need to organise a PolSA and a larger search team. We're talking about a huge area here. Certainly, the dogs would be a good place to start. There's nothing more for us to do around here, so we'll go back, and I'll speak to the boss and see if we can deploy further resources."

The teams headed back to the cars. Abby and Scott decided to have a drive around the local area to see if they could spot anything unusual.

Scott parked. As he and Abby sat inside, he overheard some comments amongst the crowds that had gathered.

He turned to Abby. "What do you notice with that lot?"

Abby glanced over at the residents nudging each other and nattering away with smiles on their faces.

"Well, they don't seem to be that bothered about a body being discovered on their doorstep."

Scott agreed.

He singled out a comment amongst all the chatter. One of the youths remarked, "That's one less black shit."

His words were met with a cackle of laughter as the group creased up. There had been a history of racial tension in the area for many years. Feral youths, continuous antisocial behaviour, high unemployment, and poor social services had led to frustration on the estate.

The tension remained as they drove through the surrounding streets. Residents viewed them with suspicion. He sensed the atmosphere changing. Even though the estate was known for it, on this occasion, a stronger air of malice hung in the air.

Something hit the side of his car, and Scott screeched to a halt. First, he thought it was a rock or stone.

"What was that?" Abby said as she glanced around.

They both exited the car and walked around its perimeter. On the back rear quarter panel, the remnants of an egg trickled down the vehicle. Fragments of shell and yoke clung to the paintwork.

"Did you see where that came from?" Scott asked, checking up and down the street, scrutinising every front door and window for any signs of movement. Abby did the same.

"No, nothing. Just some scrotes with nothing better to do. I don't think we should hang around in case the next one isn't an egg."

3

S cott paced in the doorway as he waited for Meadows to finish his phone call. The first twenty-four hours of any case were the most crucial. With the assumption that the child had been dead less than twelve hours, time wasn't on Scott's side. His mind kept flashing back to the hideous scene he had just left.

A child, that's all it was. A boy who hadn't begun his life yet.

His mind raced as he thought about the child's final moments. Had he been scared? Had he been conscious? Had he suffered pain? How could someone be so sadistic?

Scott shook his head in disbelief. Having lost his own child, Becky, dealing with infant and child deaths always hit too close to home. The cases clouded his judgement, though he didn't admit it. Seeing his own child mowed down by a reckless joyrider had caused him to question his values. Would he have been better off going on a personal vendetta to find the culprit and dishing out his own brand of vigilante justice?

He had tried to stay on the right side of the law and left it to his colleagues to investigate the case. When they had drawn a blank, his trust and belief in the system had shattered into a thousand pieces, much in the same way that his life had.

He was dragged away from his darkest thoughts when he heard his name being called. Meadows waved him in.

"I've watched the body-cam footage from Abby. It doesn't look good from where I'm sitting. What do we have?"

Scott shook his head in agreement with Meadows's initial assessment as he took a seat across the table from his boss.

"It's very grim, sir. We're looking at a child between the age of five and seven. The victim has been mutilated. The head has been removed, along with the arms. No evidence of them in the immediate vicinity. The murderer also sliced down the chest, exposing the internal organs. Dr Hall didn't find any other visible injuries apart from those."

Meadows grimaced. "I hope the poor kid wasn't alive when he went through that."

"I'm afraid he was, sir. There's significant blood loss. That suggests he was alive. Whether he was conscious or not is a different matter."

Meadows rolled his eyes. "Just what we need. The local press will have a field day. The fact it's a child means they'll be all over this case. And we'll have panicked parents everywhere."

Scott nodded and shrugged. "Is it worth putting out a press release?"

"No, not yet. Not until we have a few more facts and an identity."

"I'm suggesting that we organise a PolSA and search team, sir."

"It's a big draw on resources, Scott. What's your reasoning behind the request?"

"Because it's a large search area and because the boy's head and limbs are still missing. They could be close by.

Combining a search team with the dogs may help us to cover the area quicker."

Scott understood Meadows's hesitation. Putting a PolSA team together – comprising a police search adviser trained to plan and manage search activity, as well as uniform, search-trained officers – took resources away from other jobs.

Meadows agreed and made a call to organise a PolSA team, to be made available as soon as a risk assessment had been made. The team would still report in to the SIO, who had overall control of the case.

"Anything else?" Meadows asked.

"Other than the old gentleman who found him, eyewitnesses are thin on the ground. We hardly get on with some of the Whitehawk residents. There's a reluctance to talk to us. And something didn't feel right when Abby and I were there."

Meadows narrowed his eyes and pursed his lips. "What do you mean?"

Scott paused for a moment, trying to find the right words to describe his gut feeling.

"I can't put my finger on it, sir. There was an uneasy atmosphere as Abby and I drove around the streets. Just this palpable tension. It was unnerving."

"Well, that just may be because a body has been found. People are cautious and tense. They wonder if they're next, or did they know the person killed, or worse, does the killer live amongst them. Most don't expect it to happen on their doorstep, so maybe that's why there's this unusual tension?"

"Erm, maybe, but I'm not too sure." Scott rose from his seat. "The PM is scheduled for later this afternoon. As soon as I know more, I'll give you an update."

"Do that, Scott. I need to report up the chain as soon as possible."

SCOTT PULLED up a seat alongside Abby and briefed her on his meeting with Meadows.

Abby tidied her paperwork. "I've been going through the MisPer reports for the last few weeks. There's nothing about a missing child of that age. The last report we had was about three weeks ago when a white eight-year-old girl went missing. Wrong sex and wrong IC. Shall I look back further?"

"Incidentally, what happened with that case?" Scott asked.

Abby checked her notes. "The parents are separated. The mum is the legal guardian, and the dad failed to return his daughter on one of his days."

"Okay. It makes sense to go back a few more weeks just to double-check. But generally, if a child of this age goes missing, then someone would report it. A young child goes missing and the parents don't come forward? I don't buy that."

"Unless something happened to the parents?" Abby suggested.

That was another thought that had crossed Scott's mind. In his experience, if a child went missing and the parents hadn't reported it, it was often the uncles, aunties, grandparents, or even their school or nursery who would contact the police.

"Listen, Abby, can you hold the fort for a little bit? All this stuff with the kid...it made me realise I haven't been to see Becky and Tina for a while. I could do with stopping by there before I head to the PM. Can I meet you at the morgue?"

Abby's face softened. "Yes, sorry. I... I know this must be hard for you. You go, and I'll keep an eye on things. If anything comes up, I'll phone you. But I'll see you later."

Scott squeezed Abby's arm in thanks.

Abby called after him as he walked off. "Hey. Take it easy. I'm here if you need me."

Scott gave Abby the smallest of smiles before he turned and left.

———

IT FELT like an eternity since his last visit. Pangs of guilt twisted his insides and threatened to drown him in pain once again. Like moody clouds on a winter's day, his inner darkness had refused to budge for so long. They had trailed after him, day and night, for years. Persistent. Haunting.

In recent months the grief had shifted. It used to have a vice-like grip around his throat that would suffocate him with panic and fear. But no longer.

A turn of seasons heralded a change in Angel's Corner. Leaves from the surrounding trees had lost their grip on branches, falling to the ground and settling amongst the gravestones, to cover the area in a soft blanket. Scott knelt and picked them away, along with a few weeds that appeared amongst the blades of grass.

"I think of you every day, little one. I imagine what you'd be like now. You'd be tearing up the place, pitting your mum against me, and finding lots of ways to curl me around your little finger." He laughed; the sound wasn't as hollow as in past visits. "And you would have. I just know I would have been too soft with you. You'd get away with anything. *Everything.* It will soon be Christmas, and I'm sure you'd already have your wish list ready for Santa." Scott sighed. "Just because you're not here, it doesn't mean I don't think of you."

A lump lodged in his throat. His eyes watered as he stared at the little picture of Becky set into the headstone. "I promise I will bring you a Christmas present. From me and Mummy." He brushed his thumb against her picture.

Scott brought his eyes level with the horizon, wiping his tears away with the back of his hand. He gazed around this small corner of the cemetery. *So many young lives taken so quickly.*

His mind shifted to the young victim they had discovered that morning. Where were the parents grieving over their lost child?

Someone out there must know who he is. Someone must miss him.

Scott stood and brushed dirt off his knees. He placed two fingers on his lips and planted a kiss on Becky's picture. "I promise I won't leave it as long next time."

A part of him wanted to remain there, to feel connected with his daughter. If he had a choice, he'd sit there all day, every day, just to escape the cruel world that lay beyond the cemetery. He stopped at Tina's grave next to spend a quiet moment before making his way to the mortuary.

4

A sombre-looking Neil showed Scott and Abby through to the examination room. On previous visits, Cara's assistant would have greeted them with a smile. They would have chatted about trivial things as they made their way from the entrance to the robing area and then through to the examination room. On this occasion, the presence of a child had left a sad, indelible mark on the whole mortuary team.

As Scott and Abby walked into the room, they saw Cara with her face positioned three or four inches away from the cadaver. Her bright, cheerful disposition was absent from this particular post-mortem. She puffed out her cheeks and stepped back when they joined her at the table.

The child's body took up a third of the steel table. In the cold clinical surroundings of the examination room, a reverent silence filled the air as all three stared at the remains. No one exchanged glances. No words were spoken.

Abby wrapped one arm around her waist and brought her other hand to her mouth. A mixture of shock, sadness, and revulsion was etched on her face. Her eyes widened.

Scott swallowed hard. Thankfully, he'd attended less than a handful of post-mortems involving children. But on this occasion, the sight of a child's body without its arms and head only reminded him again of the horrific crime. He stared at the spot where the child's head should have been.

"This ranks as one of those occasions when I most hate my job." He glanced at Cara, who had pursed her lips in sympathy. "Let's get this over and done with. What can you tell us?"

Neil stood by Cara's side, holding a clipboard that detailed the findings so far.

Cara said, "We have a clean cut to the neck, most likely done with a very large, very sharp knife. As suspected, there are no serrated edges to the skin. That confirms that the head wasn't cut in a sawing motion. There's significant blood loss, which suggests that the child was alive when that happened."

Scott nodded.

"The removal of the arms hasn't been done as cleanly. The initial cuts *were* clean, but when we looked closer at the bone structures in the shoulder, a more destructive force had been applied. It appears that whoever carried this out found it difficult to separate the arms from the body. I found chop marks on the bone."

Cara grabbed her scalpel and indicated where the bones appeared to have splintered and broken into smaller fragments.

She continued, "What is concerning is that the child's heart was removed, hence why the chest cavity was opened."

"Oh, Jesus!" Abby muttered.

"Has anything else been removed?" Scott asked.

Cara shook her head. "No, nothing. There's a lot of disturbance to the internal organs. It's as if the killer was rummaging around inside."

Scott took a sharp intake of air and tutted. "Was there any...?" He looked down at the boy's lower half.

"No. There's no evidence of sexual interference," Cara said.

Scott let out a sigh of relief.

She continued with her feedback. "Identification will take longer. Without the presence of the arms and head, fingerprints and dental records are out of the question. I've taken some blood samples so we can get a DNA profile. We'll send those through to the lab right away. I've also extracted the stomach contents so they can be examined. Generally, he was a well-nourished boy. I've speculated on the extra weight that his arms and head would carry, and I believe he was of average weight and well cared for. If you want, I can call in a paediatric pathologist to see if I've missed anything?"

"No, I think that's fine for the moment. We need to see how our investigation proceeds first," Scott replied.

"What are these?" Abby was pointing at some marks on the boy's torso.

Cara moved along the table to where Abby stood. "It's scarring. And it's not recent either. Three scars about an inch long and half a centimetre apart, all equidistant. I've seen this type of scarring before, but it's usually found on the facial cheeks. Common in African tribal communities. But that's as far as my knowledge goes."

Scott stepped forward and inspected the scarring for his own benefit. "Without formal identification, is there any way for us to determine his background, his origins – that type of thing?"

Cara nodded. "Sometimes, we can identify the country of origin due to advances in forensic science that allow us to extract mineral samples from the bones. We cross-reference them against the various drinking waters found across the globe. It would depend on how long he's been in this country.

But we can look into that and speak to Matt in forensic services?"

"I doubt those scars would have been inflicted on a UK-born African child," Scott suggested. "Well, it's worth a punt. It depends on how detailed the analysis is, and how long it takes. But I certainly think the country of origin could play a part in this and help us to build a bigger picture of his background."

Cara agreed. "It can certainly be useful if, as in this case, the individual is from another country. Perhaps they've not been reported as missing because they are here illegally. Or because there are no other means of identification."

Scott's eyes widened. He pointed at Cara. "You've just hit on an important point."

Cara looked puzzled. "Have I?"

"He could be an illegal, which is why no one's reported him missing. His parents are too scared."

Abby shrugged in agreement.

Cara said, "His last meal appears to have been nuts, raisins, and some type of white, sticky substance. The process by which food is absorbed into the body can take anything from twenty-two hours to two days to complete. Within that time, food is broken down and reduced to a liquid pulp before absorption. The nuts and raisins have hardly been broken down, so he certainly had his last meal within twenty-two hours of his death."

"Seriously? You can determine that?" Abby asked. She looked surprised by the level of detail Cara could determine.

"Absolutely. Advances in technology and forensic science have helped us to look at a victim like never before. We can identify the circumstances around their death, their environment, and their habits, just by examining the stomach contents."

"I didn't think we could go so deep."

Cara smiled. "So yes, stomach contents can be a treasure trove of information. We can reveal if the deceased was experimenting with any form of drug or food that might have brought about a state of internal poisoning. It can reveal anything like trace elements of poisons or other toxins that might not be found in the deceased's blood system."

Scott said, "We'll shoot off now. It sounds like you have plenty to be getting on with. Call me if there's anything else you identify that can't wait until you submit your report."

Cara nodded and returned to continue her examination.

Scott headed for the doors with Abby following.

IN THE CAFÉ, Scott stared into his black Americano while Abby sipped on her soya latte. It was one of those rare occasions where they sat in silence, both reflecting on the situation. Seeing the boy's body had left them both saddened and traumatised.

Scott broke the silence. "You would think that we'd get used to post-mortems, considering the number we've been to. But they always have a knack of throwing a curveball at you. I think what I've just seen is as bad as it gets."

Abby hummed a reply and returned to her drink.

It was a further few minutes before Abby said, "Do you know that this is the first post-mortem I've been to with you where you haven't stuffed your face the moment we left?"

A small smile broke on Scott's face. He huffed. "Do you blame me?"

They both shared a light-hearted moment before shaking off the melancholy and calling it a day.

5

The usual chatter, banter, and frivolity were absent the following morning as the team sat in an arc around the incident board. Scott had pinned the SOCO's photographs on the whiteboard. A feeling of loss dominated as everyone stared at the dismembered body of the child.

Scott glanced around the team, looking from one team member to another. "Okay, you've all seen these pictures, and you've read the initial report from Dr Hall following the post-mortem that Abby and I attended yesterday late afternoon."

He then summarised the main points of the post-mortem back to the team.

"Do you have any indication whether the child was conscious at the point of dismemberment?" Raj asked.

"No, we haven't at the moment. That he was alive at all is bad enough," Scott replied. "How did you get on with the door to door?"

Raj flicked through his notes. "Feedback from the house-to-house enquiries was poor, to be honest, guv. In most instances, we were met with a wall of silence. No one saw anything, and no one heard anything. I sensed it was a case of, 'It's none of my business, so I don't get involved.' There were a few derogatory remarks about us, and a general unwillingness to talk to us."

Helen picked up from where Raj ended. "There were a few racist comments as well, guv, which Raj and I cautioned them about, but we just had a mouthful of abuse."

Scott had expected this and had held out little hope for support and intelligence from the local community. They often viewed the police with suspicion, so the chances of gathering anything of value was slim.

Raj narrowed his eyes. "There were a few African families, but again no one willing to talk to us. It was crazy," he said, shaking his head. "The door would open just a fraction, we'd see a set of eyes darting back and forth between me and Helen, and then the occupant would shake their head and shut the door. Uniform were given the same response."

"Okay, Raj. That's helpful to know," Scott said. "Can you contact social services and find out how many African families live on the Whitehawk estate that are under their care? Find out their residential status, and what type of support structures are in place for them. Now we don't know if this child came from the Whitehawk, Brighton, or even Sussex. For all we know, the child could have come from a different part of the country. So we're scratching around in the dark for the moment."

"That might be the case, guv," Mike added. "Bearing in mind the post-mortem said he'd been dead for less than twelve hours, if he had been killed in a different part of the country and dumped on the Whitehawk, it would need to have been a quick journey."

"Perhaps. The child could have been alive, brought down from a different part of the country, and then killed either at or close to the crime scene. That would be the more logical explanation and would fit in with the timeline of death. We deployed a PolSA team last night, and they are continuing their search again this morning with the help of dogs. Again it's a long shot, but we need to be thorough."

"Have they found anything yet?" an officer near the back asked.

Scott shook his head. "No, nothing yet. I'm hoping that the remaining body parts might have been dumped close by, and we need those to help us with identification. Or hopefully they locate anything else relating to the murder, including the murder weapon."

"I'm still checking the MisPer reports, and nothing flashes up of black children missing locally or within Sussex." Abby blew out a breath. "Someone must have lost their child or reported it to someone unless this is a cover-up. I'm drawing a blank so far. That's why we need to go to the press."

"But we have little to give them."

"Surely a press appeal might flush something out?"

Scott agreed with Abby's suggestion. It was something that he was keen to discuss with Meadows.

"I'll chase up Matt for any forensics results that they have so far, but at the moment it's a waiting game," he said. "We also need to look at whether there were any reasons the body was dumped in that specific area. Random or intentional? Does that location have any significance? Was the body taken there because it could be concealed easily? Go back to our records and check for similar crimes." Scott tracked back through his own memories. "I can't think of any, so we may need to go back a bit further. Look at any local paedophiles on the register. Are there any who have displayed a violent tendency or fantasised about killing and dismembering children?"

Everyone went still and stared at Scott. He paced in front of the incident board as he stroked his chin.

"I'm also curious as to why the body was dismembered. The natural conclusion is the killer was attempting to remove the most obvious signs of identification. But is there anything else to it? And why the removal of the child's heart?"

The others nodded and made notes.

Scott continued, "In all my years of service, I've never come across a case where any victim, adult or child, has had their heart removed. So that's another crucial point we need to examine. If anyone has theories or ideas about any of this, then make sure you share it here as soon as possible. It's going to be difficult identifying the victim without a facial image, dental records, or prints. So for the time being, we'll have to rely on a DNA profile when it comes through."

Abby chipped in, "I'll check with the NCA. It's a particular MO. The removal of the heart, the head, and the arms – that must be key. It would be interesting to know if the NCA has identified similar cases in the past."

Scott pointed at her with his pen. "Good call, Abby. Can you lead on that?"

Abby nodded.

Mike had already started compiling a list of African community centres, churches, and support groups that the team could explore. Scott had suggested that he add primary schools to the list in case a child had been reported as an unexplained absence.

The team understood the importance of solving this case, firstly because the victim was a child, and secondly, because of the heinous nature of the crime.

SCOTT LEFT the team to follow all the lines of enquiry. He headed off to the drinks machine to grab himself a not-so-desirable black Americano before returning to his desk.

Something that Cara had mentioned during their visit to the mortuary had sparked his interest. He pulled up Google Images and typed in African tribal scars. He wasn't too sure what he was looking for, but with very little evidence and no clear motive to go on, he was willing to follow up every hunch, idea, and scrap of evidence.

A bewildering array of facial scarrings returned in the results. He sat open-mouthed as he stared at them. Many surprised him. They weren't as grotesque as he'd expected, but rather intricate and artistically created scarring patterns.

Some patterns looked like exaggerated crease lines on the forehead; others looked like marijuana leaves. They weren't, but that was the best way to describe them. A few resembled the three lines of scars that had been discovered on the boy's body. Then there were extreme examples: tiny scars that resembled dots, covering at least eighty per cent of the person's face.

He flicked back a page and explored the procedures in detail. Scarring was a common practice in many African countries, including Sudan, Ethiopia, Nigeria, South Africa, and the Congo. He discovered that each particular style of scarring had its own name. Styles like Pele, Owu, Abaja, and Gombo leapt out from the page and were often used to identify a person's tribe, family or patrilineal heritage, and for beautification.

"Beautification...not sure about that," he murmured. Scott hadn't realised that such markings were regarded as a thing of beauty in some cultures.

His eyes narrowed as he read a line outlining how scars were inscribed on the body by burning or cutting the skin during childhood.

Scott leant back in his chair and reflected on what he'd seen. This wasn't a practice he knew much about, but from what he had read so far, scarring had been going on through African nations for generations. It even had a formal name: scarification.

A low hum of conversations echoed through the canteen as Abby grabbed a cup of tea and a packet of crisps. Amid the constant coming and going of officers, staff sat in huddles. Several officers preferred their own company and sat farther away from the crowds, reading a book or magazine. It was a place for officers to unwind and de-stress before tackling the next interview, the next call-out, or the reams of paperwork that needed to be completed for every case.

Abby preferred her own company and often sought out an empty table where she could chill. She wasn't interested in hearing about the station gossip or the latest drunken hook-up on a night out. Nor could she tolerate the open flirting between colleagues who spent too much time together.

Abby leant back and stretched, feeling the bones in her spine crack. A wave of relief flooded through her body.

Samantha Huxtable, a uniformed colleague that Abby knew well, strode over to her. A keen runner, Samantha had entered many half-marathons with Abby. With their differing shift patterns, they rarely had opportunities to bump into each other at the station.

She sat down opposite a smiling Abby.

"Hi, Abby. It's been ages since I've seen you. Sounds like you guys have been busy?"

Abby rolled her eyes. "Is there a time that we're never busy? Take last Wednesday, for example. Supposed to finish at ten p.m., but I ended up finishing at three a.m. because we had a prisoner in. I was on the phone to CPS for more than two hours. But at least we charged him and have another scumbag off the streets."

Samantha offered a sympathetic smile as she tied her blonde hair up into a ponytail. She had a fair complexion and a thin face with high cheekbones. Years of running had given her a lean, muscular frame.

"What are you working on at the moment?" Abby asked.

"Bit of a weird one, but then is there anything that isn't weird in our jobs?" She shrugged with a look of exasperation. "Would you believe it, but I'm dealing with a series of petnappings in and around Brighton. As if I haven't better things to do?"

Abby rolled her eyes. "We have people moaning that there aren't enough uniformed officers on the street, and now they have you looking for pets?"

Samantha nodded. "Two cats, one small Yorkie, a chicken, and seventy-four-year-old Doris's pussy."

Abby choked on her tea. They both let out a roar of laughter before carrying on with their catch-up.

SCOTT HAD BEEN in management meetings for over three hours before he returned to his desk, sank into his chair and let out a mighty groan. He threw his notepad across the desk, along with his lunch – a ham and cheese sandwich. If there was one thing he hated about his job, it was the endless meetings that came with the grade. Budgets, staffing levels, crime reduction rates, cases solved, plus all the overinflated egos pushing their own agenda.

The fact was that the thin blue line was becoming thinner as each year passed. Meadows's comment about the budgetary cuts had reminded him of that fact.

Abby poked her head around the door moments after Scott returned. "Heavy session?"

Scott waved at her, too tired to even open his mouth. He leant forward and twisted the top off his water bottle, then took a long, slow glug. "My mind is frazzled. My body wants to crawl under this desk and sleep for an hour."

Abby laughed. "Hey, listen. I thought that maybe we should all get together for dinner. Jonathon has heard so much about you and Cara. He's the one who suggested getting together for a bite to eat one night. What do you think?"

Scott narrowed his eyes and gave her a teasing smile. "This all sounds grown-up for you. Is this so we can discuss your wedding plans?"

Abby blushed and crossed her arms. She then pointed in Scott's direction. "I'm warning you. Just one call to Cara and I'll get all the meaty gossip about your holiday."

Scott rocked back in his chair. "You won't stop holding that one over me, will you?"

Abby shot him a mischievous grin that suggested, *Try me.*

He added, "Yeah, why not? I'm shooting off soon, so I'll speak to Cara about it this evening. You can come over to mine though. If we came to yours, we wouldn't get much more than a cheese sandwich and a lettuce leaf."

Abby groaned.

He smiled. "It should be interesting, two coppers, a

pathologist, and an optician. I'm sure there's a joke in there somewhere but can't think of one. I'll get back to you with some dates."

———

THE HEAVY SMELL of vinegar wafted up from their plates as Scott and Cara finished off a fish and chip supper in front of the TV. Both were too tired to cook. The last two days had taken it out of them, and their holiday felt like nothing more than a distant memory.

They had enjoyed the holiday so much that they were already talking about another break in the same area in the spring of next year. Cara had moaned that a year was too long. She suggested a short break in January to the Canary Islands for some warm winter sun might just be the tonic for them.

Scott liked the idea, even more so knowing that Cara was already thinking long term about them.

Cara was excited at the prospect of hosting a dinner party. She commented that it would be fun to have a night off with good company and good food. Scott hesitated, knowing what Cara and Abby were like when they were together. The thought of them colluding and ganging up on him filled him with dread. He could just picture the laughter.

Discussing plans for a dinner party with friends. It felt natural, normal, and was something thousands of couples did up and down the country on a Friday or Saturday night. Simple pleasures like that had been missing from his life for the last few years. He was beginning to understand why his life had felt so empty.

He and Cara had already reached a friendly impasse over the evening's menu. She was in favour of pâté for starters. Scott disagreed and wanted something more substantial like fishcakes. Cara thought chicken would be good for a main, whereas Scott thought something heartier like a boeuf bourguignon would be better. The difference of opinions raged on and off for most of the evening.

Cara had moved her plate away and was stretching out on the sofa, resting her head on Scott's lap. With a bottle of Peroni in one hand, and his other hand caressing Cara's arm, he continued to put forward his case for his chosen dishes. He paused when he realised that he had been speaking without interruption – a rarity whilst talking to Cara.

He glanced down to see Cara was asleep. He smiled and stroked her hair. He studied her facial features, her firm full lips, her long eyelashes, and high cheekbones. Dark trestles of hair wrapped around her face and lay in the crook of her neck. She was beautiful in every way, and not just her feminine curves and large breasts that made her even more attractive. Scott couldn't believe his luck as he gazed down at her. She made him smile, she made him laugh, and she made him feel wanted.

As he watched her in repose, a little more of the gaping hole in his heart filled with love.

7

T he next morning hadn't started well for Scott. The PolSA team had drawn a blank, finding no evidence of the missing limbs, a murder weapon, or anything to push the case forward. Various other items of interest had been discovered, such as a claw hammer, a small kitchen knife, and a small paring knife. These items had been bagged up and sent away for analysis.

Scott had put a call through to Meadows requesting that the PolSA team continue their search for another day. Meadows had argued that the cost far outweighed the benefit, as the officers needed to be redeployed back to their teams. After some coercing from Scott, Meadows had relented and agreed that the search could continue until six p.m. that evening.

Frustration infiltrated every cell in Scott's body, tensing his muscles into rigid fibres of annoyance. He had hoped to deploy the PolSA team sooner, out of fear any evidence could have degraded or been removed. But there wasn't much point in thinking about such missed opportunities now. The fact

that the PolSA team had drawn a blank disappointed him
more.

Scott's irritation with politics and procedures heightened
when Meadows confirmed that CC Lennon and DCC
Grayling were still discussing the merits of a TV appeal at
this early stage in the investigation. They had expressed
concern that they didn't want to cause any unnecessary panic
amongst the community. Scott understood their argument,
but in reality, he knew their reluctance to go public was based
on ghosts from the past.

Back in 1986, two nine-year-old children went missing
whilst playing. Their bodies were found the following day in
Wild Park, Moulsecoomb. The case became known as *The
Babes in the Woods Murders*, which attracted nationwide interest. With a conviction not forthcoming for the abduction and
murders until many years later, the tragedy had left a deep
scar in the minds of Brightonians.

It had also placed Brighton on the map for all the wrong
reasons. The police had come under fire at the time, and
many questioned why the killer, central to one of Brighton's
most haunting unsolved crimes, had escaped justice for so
long.

Despite Lennon and Grayling's objection, Scott knew the
significant value of a press appeal. Messages could be crafted,
the aim to update the public, but also to help the investigation gain new evidence and develop lines of inquiry.

In Scott's opinion, there were three key benefits by which
media appeals could help his investigation. The first was a
straightforward appeal for witnesses. The second was if he
needed to rule someone close to the victim in or out of his
investigation. Finally, it sometimes helped to provoke a reaction from the suspect. He had made his argument to
Meadows using the first option.

Scott knew that once details of the murder became public

knowledge, there would be a greater need for reassurance. Parents would want reassurance that someone was in control, and that there was hands-on leadership on the ground.

For this reason, he needed to ensure that messages during the appeal for information were equally balanced with messages of reassurance.

8

The prospect of seeing the organ torn apart and dissected excited him. Such desires had been a part of his life for as long as he could remember. A perverse fascination consumed him. He craved knowledge of how different components of a body worked together to create a living being.

He licked his lips in anticipation. His pupils dilated; his pulse throbbed in his neck. A slight sweat glistened on his forehead.

He picked up a thin-bladed knife and grasped the cold steel handle. A slight tremor shook his hand, an indicator of the elation that stirred within him. He ran the tip of the blade down the centre of the heart. The last few remnants of blood held within the organ oozed out and stained the blade a velvety red.

His smile widened. The sensations he felt were far exceeding his expectations.

He separated the two halves of the muscle and examined the intricate internal structure, mentally noting everything he'd seen in a book. No matter how many times he'd carried out this exact procedure, it always felt so new, so exciting, and so sacred.

This would be the first of many opportunities to practise his craft, to hone his skills, and offer a sacrifice in the way Xabi had. He glanced over his right shoulder and nodded. The small stack of clear Tupperware containers held his rich trophies. Each organ was being cradled in its own bath of red, sticky goodness, the elixir of life.

He turned to the left and stared at the small child asleep on a blanket. A young boy who'd spent far too long here already. The boy slept hard. The herbs that had been mixed in with his food ensured he did. In the beginning, he had cried. Cried too much, in fact, to the point where the man could no longer tolerate the child's constant moaning one more second. He preferred to work in silence.

But it would soon be over for the little boy. His time was near.

9

A s with most cases that Scott managed, he reverted to his trusted notepad and pen. He had written *BOY* in capitals in the centre of his blank page. From there, he had drawn out a line to another balloon box, which said no head or arms. By the side of that box he placed a question mark. As yet, he was uncertain as to the motive for the dismemberment. He drew another short line away from the central theme, and at the end of it he wrote *Ritual killing? Paedophile?*

Maybe it was just a monster without a soul.

A motive for the killing was still largely unknown, along with any significance of the location where the body had been found. In the early stages of any murder investigation, the team usually faced more questions than answers. Hopefully, the different lines of enquiries that the team were chasing down would give them some clarity.

Another thing also played on Scott's mind. If the child hadn't been reported missing, had harm come to his parents?

A heavy rapping on his open door vibrated the walls and jolted Scott from his thoughts. Mike filled the doorway, waving his notepad. There was nothing delicate about Mike. A knock on the door with his thick knuckles hit as hard as a regular person's closed fist.

"What's up, Mike?"

"I've been following up all those avenues that we spoke about at the briefing. So far, I've drawn a blank with community centres and support groups, but I still have a few to work through on the list. But I had two interesting conversations. The first is with Down's Nursery. They have a young lad aged four who hasn't been in for over five days. There's been no answer from the parents either. I did say to the nursery that we were perhaps looking for a child a little older. But the nursery nurse I spoke to added that the lad in question was quite a large lad for his age and towered above the others. She said you could mistake him for being five or six years old."

Mike flicked through his spiral-bound notepad. As he recapped his notes, Scott listened, tapping the end of his pen on the desk in a mixture of frustration and curiosity.

"Then we have Oakwood Primary School," Mike continued. "They have a young child who's been absent from school for three days. He's an African boy aged six years old. So he certainly matches the age, sex, and race of the young lad that we found. I have an address of where the parents are staying. And the interesting thing is they are asylum seekers from South Africa, staying in council-owned property on the Whitehawk."

MIKE AND SCOTT set off with some urgency to visit both of the residential addresses given by the nursery and the primary school. Mike continued to give Scott further updates as they made their way to an address off Coldean Lane. The property was only five minutes away from Down's Nursery. The manager of the nursery had been concerned enough after three days to pay a visit to the house. Unfortunately, her visit had been futile. She had peered through the letter box but saw nothing untoward, and reached the conclusion that perhaps they had moved on or had left the country.

According to Down's Nursery, Mbali and Samuel Sibeko, parents of four-year-old Yaseen, lived inside. Scott and Mike had stopped off at Down's Nursery first, and they had acquired a photograph of the boy that the nursery had on file. Mike removed a small navy sweatshirt with the nursery emblem from the clothes hook for Yaseen and placed it in an evidence bag. It would be sent to forensics and used to build a DNA profile for crossmatching with the victim.

Scott rapped on the door several times whilst Mike walked around the front of the terraced property. He cupped his hands around his eyes and peered in through the windows. Scott crouched down and lifted the letter box flap. There were no circulars piling up on the doormat, there were no sounds, and there were none of the odious smells that would suggest that the inhabitants had come to harm.

"Anything?" Scott asked.

Mike shook his head. "Nope, diddly-squat. From what I can see, it looks clean in there. Not much furniture. Looks sparse. Typical council property."

Mike checked with the neighbours on either side. Residents hadn't seen the family for over a week. Initial feedback suggested that the family were friendly and polite but quiet. Other than saying hello to them on the street, residents had had little to do with them. The family had been in the property for six months.

Mike made a mental note before moving on to the next location to check with the council about previous addresses and any indication of their current whereabouts.

10

Scott had been keen to move to the next location, but Mike insisted on stopping to grab a quick burger, muffins, and a cup of tea. He devoured his lunch in the car.

"Keep your window open," Scott said as they went to exit the car. "It smells like a greasy chippy in here."

Mike grumbled to himself as he gulped down the remnants of his tea. "Well, you were the one who said you were in a hurry. Otherwise, I would have sat outside the car and eaten it. By the way, the double choc chip muffins went down a treat with this cuppa." Mike lifted his polystyrene cup up to Scott.

Scott shook his head and walked up the garden path. He was back in familiar territory again, the Whitehawk estate. A typical council property, it had dirty brown pebble-dashed walls and a small patch of overgrown grass that passed as a front garden. Weeds crept up through the cracks in the broken concrete path.

Nothing more than flimsy green wire fencing served as the front fence. It was cheap budget fencing that people often used to form demarcation lines between them and neighbouring properties.

The sound of raised voices from within caused Mike and Scott to pause by the front door. They could make out a heated exchange. A female with a high-pitched scream was matched in equal proportions by a heavy, deep male voice raised in anger.

Mike rolled his eyes. "If this is a domestic, then I'm walking. Uniform can deal with it."

Scott's chest rose and fell as he took a deep breath. He pursed his lips before knocking.

The voices inside quieted. Scott fully expected someone to come to the door, but after a short pause, with no answer, he knocked harder.

"Hello? It's the police." He could make out the faint scurrying of footsteps and some commotion inside. The footsteps became louder and stopped behind the door before the sound of a key turned in the lock.

A short, broad black man answered the door. With the door ajar only six inches, Scott saw a round face with a large flat nose. His hair had been tightly cropped. He offered the broadest of smiles, which accentuated his chubby cheeks. His eyes shifted between the two strangers on the doorstep.

Scott and Mike held up their warrant cards. "I'm Detective Inspector Baker; this is my colleague Detective Constable Wilson. We are looking for Anneke and Patrick Chauke. We believe they live here?"

The man opened the door wider but continued to fix his gaze upon the two officers. Scott and Mike could see the full figure of the man. He was squat and rotund, dressed in a smart, dark navy suit, with a white, granddad-collar-style shirt. Mike noticed his seventies-looking black shiny patent shoes.

In a heavy accent, he addressed them. "I'm afraid they don't live here."

Mike and Scott exchanged the briefest of glances. "Who lives here?"

The man hesitated; then his eyes narrowed. "May I ask what this is in regard to?"

"And you are?"

"I am Joshua Mabunda, *Pastor* Joshua Mabunda."

"And you live here?"

The man shook his head. Scott felt they were going around in circles.

"So what is your connection with the family who lives here?"

The pastor remained tight-lipped as he stared at the two men. Scott lurched forward, about to take a firmer stance, when he heard the soft sound of two people speaking from somewhere within the house.

"Can you tell me who lives here, sir?" Mike asked. He took a step closer to the doorway to signal his demand for an answer.

The pastor opened his mouth to reply when the two voices from behind him became louder. A man and woman stepped into the hallway from a back room. They spoke to the pastor in soft tones, in a language that neither Scott nor Mike understood.

The couple were dressed in simple clothes. The man wore a creased white T-shirt, light blue jeans, and brown sandals. The female with him wore an orange, African dashiki print loose dress that hung off her thin frame.

"Are either of you Anneke or Patrick Chauke?" Scott asked, looking past the pastor.

The couple remained tight-lipped. The man draped a protective arm around the shoulder of the woman. The woman had a pained expression on her face. Fear widened her eyes. With a pained expression, she glanced between the pastor and the officers.

"This is Anneke and Patrick Chauke. They do not speak English, and I speak on their behalf." The pastor turned towards the couple and muttered something that caused them to retreat half a step.

"What language do they speak?" Scott asked.

"They speak Isi Zulu. Anything you wish to ask them, you ask me, and I will relay it for you."

Scott's jaw tightened in frustration. "Do they have a son?"

Without a look in their direction, the pastor nodded. "They do."

"And what is their son's name?"

"Michael."

"And how old is Michael?"

The pastor gazed at both officers. Even though the man was calm, his eyes appeared lifeless and lacking emotion. The absence of an answer began to grate on both Mike and Scott.

Scott raised his eyebrows as if to suggest *Well?*

"Six."

"And where is he?"

Before the pastor could reply, the woman in the corridor moaned. Tears flooded her eyes. "My babeee. Where is my baby?"

"I thought you said they couldn't speak English," Scott said in a firm tone.

Unease hung in the air as the pastor shifted his gaze to the floor. Mike looked at Scott, teeth clenched. Scott shook his head. The last thing he needed was his officer dragging the pastor out by his collar.

Anneke came rushing towards the door, Patrick just inches behind her. "Have you found my baby?"

"Michael?" Scott asked.

She nodded. Her teary eyes searched both men for answers.

"When was the last time you saw him?"

"Three days ago," replied Patrick.

"Does your son have any distinguishing features?" Scott asked.

The father nodded. "He has a red birthmark that covers the entire sole of his right foot."

"Any other features?"

Patrick thought for a few moments before adding that his son had three distinct, short scars on his abdomen.

Scott and Mike glanced at each other. The two features that the father had described matched those discovered during the post-mortem.

Patrick dropped his head; his bottom lip quivered with emotion. He glanced at his wife. Her eyes expressed the excruciating pain they both clearly felt, grief threatening to swallow them into a dark vortex. "Have you found my son?"

Scott cleared his throat. "We've discovered the body of a young child. The distinguishing marks that you mentioned are consistent with those that we found on the body."

Anneke Chauke dropped to her knees and buried her head in her hands as she wailed and sobbed. Patrick knelt down beside her and cradled her in his arms. Anneke buried her head in his chest. After a few tense moments, her cries fell silent.

"I want to see my child," Patrick demanded through teary eyes and a stiff jaw.

Scott stepped forward and dropped to one knee. He placed one hand on Patrick's shoulder.

"I'm afraid that's not possible at the moment. There are some tests that are still being conducted on the body." In situations like this, Scott had to lie. There was no way that any person, let alone a parent, should see a loved one after they had been the victim of such a hideous crime.

Patrick searched Scott's eyes for more information, but a gentle shake of Scott's head told Patrick that he couldn't divulge more.

Mike stayed by the front door to contain the scene.

Pastor Mabunda wore a stern expression on his face. Scott noticed that the man's eyes were boring into the parents, as if annoyed that his instructions to remain quiet had been disobeyed.

Something didn't feel right to Scott. For someone calling himself a pastor, a man of God, his demeanour suggested otherwise. His eyes were cold, his words measured, and his influence on the parents chilling.

To the parents, he whispered in a soft tone, "We'll need you to come to the station with us. We believe that the child could be your son. So we would like to ask you some questions about his disappearance and to build a better understanding of Michael. Is that okay?"

Patrick stared at Scott through heavy, swollen, sad eyes. With his shoulders sagged, he looked a broken man. Patrick was doing his hardest to be strong for his wife, holding back his emotions like a dam holding back a lake.

As he looked at Patrick, Scott felt a strong bond of empathy towards what the Chaukes were going through. The knock on the door. The presence of police officers. The news that every parent dreaded. With it so fresh, they would experience a multitude of emotions. They would be confused, frightened, and saddened. Their world had been shattered beyond belief in the same way he'd experienced.

Scott showed the parents to his car whilst Mike gathered evidence that would help them to confirm Michael's identity. He placed the boy's toothbrush in a plastic evidence bag. In separate evidence bags he placed a pillowcase from the child's bed, his pyjamas, and a T-shirt that he had worn but hadn't been washed yet.

Something about the pastor continued to trouble Scott. He had a suspicion that the pastor knew more than he was letting on, and there was a risk of not being able to locate him again if they needed to question him at a later date.

He called in uniformed officers to bring the man in for questioning. The first priority in Scott's mind was to confirm the identity of the victim and bring some closure for his parents.

11

Anneke and Patrick Chauke sat across the table from Scott and Raj. Mike and Abby were interviewing the pastor in a separate interview room down the corridor. The Chaukes held hands and sat in silence, listening to the formal introductions and cautions for the benefit of the tape recorder, with the help of an interpreter when needed.

Anneke stared at the table, unwilling to raise her eyes to meet those of the officers interviewing her. Occasional sobs racked her body every time Michael was mentioned. Though the red birthmark on the foot had identified the victim as almost certainly being their son, prior to beginning the interview, the couple had voluntarily given a buccal swab – a simple cheek swab to collect DNA. The samples could be then cross-referenced against a DNA profile of the victim for completeness.

So far Scott's questions had been answered by Patrick. His wife was too distraught to utter a word.

"What was your reason for coming to the UK?" Scott asked.

Patrick's reply was quiet. "Our villages were being perse-
cuted. We are a minority tribe. Our elders were too weak to
challenge the brutality of the marauding tribes who would
rob us, rape our women, kidnap our children, and destroy
our crops. We wanted a better life for Michael."

"And how did you get here?"

"There are people. People who can get us here. We came
across the land in a truck. We spent every bit of money we
had to get here."

"Tell me about Michael?" Scott asked.

Patrick gazed at a spot behind Scott for a few moments
before looking at Scott. "He was a fun-loving boy. Gentle,
bright, and intelligent. He wanted to do well. He would sit
there for hours looking at books."

"And when was the last time you saw him?"

Patrick shrugged his shoulders. "Three days ago. He said
he wanted to go and play in the front garden with a few other
boys. He has done that before. He must have only been gone
half an hour. When Anneke went out to call him to dinner...
he was gone." Tears squeezed from his eyes and trailed down
either side of his nose.

"So why didn't you report him missing as soon as you
couldn't find him?"

Patrick glanced at his wife. Patrick's right arm and
Anneke's left arm tensed. Scott imagined they were squeezing
hands beneath the table.

Scott leant in and rested his hands on the desk. "Listen,
we are here to help. Your son disappeared. We are awaiting
confirmation via forensic analysis, but we believe the body
that we've found is that of your son. If there's anything that
you know that will help us to identify what happened to him,
then I plead with you to tell us everything you know."

Patrick licked his lips and shifted in his chair. Even

though the room wasn't cold, he nevertheless trembled. "We went out looking for him. We knocked on a few doors of some other asylum seekers that we know. No one had seen him. We contacted the pastor, and he said he would deal with it."

Scott and Raj exchanged glances. Raj continued to make notes.

"Is there anywhere else that Michael could have gone to in the time from when he disappeared? A den, a hiding place – anything like that?"

Patrick hesitated before replying, "Pastor Mabunda organised the childminder who used to look after many children in our situation. It gave us the opportunity to meet with solicitors and support workers from the council without having to worry about Michael."

"What's the name of the childminder?"

"Margaret Eze."

"And where does Margaret live?"

Patrick shrugged. "I don't know."

Scott narrowed his eyes in confusion. "You don't know where your childminder lives?"

"No. Every time we needed her services, the pastor would come and collect Michael and take care of it. Margaret does not have her papers to stay here. She is old."

PASTOR MABUNDA SAT stony-faced in interview room two. His disposition hadn't changed from when Mike had seen him at the house. He was being just as aloof and uncooperative. Following a debrief with Scott after his interview with the parents, Mike and Abby were ready to continue questioning the pastor.

Abby sat with a pad and pen, taking notes while Mike

asked similar questions to those presented to Michael's parents. The pastor gave similar answers.

"What involvement do you have with the asylum seekers on the Whitehawk estate?"

With his arms crossed, the pastor leant back in his chair. "I'm here to help them in any way. For many, it is a scary and dangerous journey. They arrive here unsure of their outcome, wary of authority and helpless."

"And for those who arrive in this country through the human trafficking routes, you help them too?" Mike asked.

The pastor nodded. "It doesn't matter how they have come here. What matters is that they are taken care of. They are given food, shelter, and hope." His eyes lit up as he said the last word. "They want to begin new lives. They are looking for safety, good luck and fortune."

"And you help them to begin new lives?"

"That is my job. I am God's servant; I am here to do the right thing. I'm here to preach God's principles. My purpose is to show those less fortunate that even in the most destitute of times, with hope, prayers, and luck, things can turn out better."

"So when Michael went missing, why wasn't his disappearance reported immediately?" Mike probed.

"We are a community, and the children are our responsibility. It was our job to find him," he replied in a matter-of-fact manner.

"But it didn't turn out the way you had hoped for as a community..." Mike let the thought hang in the air. He changed tack. "How well do you know Margaret Eze?"

The pastor's eyes flickered as he glanced at Mike and Abby. "I know her well enough."

"When did she last see Michael?"

"I can't remember."

Mike shifted his sizeable frame and leant forward to level

his eyes with the pastor's. "You see, something doesn't really make sense. We know she's been acting as a childminder in an unofficial capacity. We also know that you've been taking Michael to her. So, are you telling me that you can't recall the last time that you took Michael to Margaret's?"

He nodded.

"For the benefit of the tape, Mr Mabunda, can you say your replies, please," Mike demanded.

"I can't remember."

Mike pushed. "Is that because you can't remember, or you're not willing to remember? Perhaps it has something to do with the fact that she's an illegal immigrant in this country? Were you involved in bringing her into this country?"

"No."

Mike tapped his pen on the table for a few moments, then asked, "May I remind you that you're under caution, Mr Mabunda. Did you have anything to do with the disappearance of Michael?"

Pastor Mabunda looked Mike squarely in the eyes. "No." His tone rang with confidence.

The interview didn't carry on for much longer. A series of questions were met with vague answers that gleaned little new information.

12

"Guv, the pastor has come back clean. He has no previous," Helen said as she updated Scott and the rest of the team around the incident board. "I'm looking into his credentials at the moment."

Scott pinned a picture of the pastor to the incident board alongside pictures of the parents and Michael. "Keep digging, Helen. Look at social security records, bank statements, and Google him. I'm not so sure about the pastor; something doesn't add up there."

"I agree, guv," Mike added. "He's keeping his cards close to his chest."

Scott agreed with Mike's assessment. "Whilst he was in the interview, we downloaded his phone records, so we can look at those."

He's definitely hiding something," Abby remarked. "I've had further information from the NCA, guv. They believe that our case has the hallmarks of a ritual killing. From their experience with ritual killings, the body is usually dismembered, in particular the removal of the head, but it's not uncommon for all the limbs to be removed. They've recorded several such incidents that bear similar hallmarks. Unfortunately, there have been no convictions."

Abby's feedback only confirmed his suspicions. Scott's search on the internet had thrown up many such cases around the world. There were just a handful in the UK, but on the African continent, there seemed to be a long history of ritual killings.

The team continued to listen to Abby's feedback. "The NCA was keen to highlight a case that attracted nationwide attention. The torso in the Thames. That was quite a complex case in London where the boy had been trafficked into the UK. He was identified as Adam."

Scott made a mental note to have a look at that case again in more detail. "I doubt any of us in this room have first-hand knowledge or a detailed understanding of ritual killings. But this case certainly points to the potential for it to be one. We have African asylum seekers in Brighton, a pastor who is not playing ball, and little intelligence to go on. This is beyond our experience. Abby, can you have a look and see if we can track down a specialist in African cultures?"

Abby nodded. "Sussex uni? I can try there first. Failing that, I can always try the School of Oriental and African Studies, which is part of the University of London."

"Good call. Mike and Raj, take the pastor back and search his place if he agrees, or apply for a search warrant if he doesn't. Take two extra officers with you. If the pastor gives you any grief, tell him that we are investigating his connection with the abduction and murder of Michael Chauke. We're looking for any evidence that Michael has been there. Organise a SOCO to accompany you." Scott clapped his hands together. "Okay, team, let's get on it. I'm off to track down the childminder."

ABBY TRAWLED through the University of Sussex website, searching for a relevant point of contact. She began by looking through the list of admin contacts but found no one who jumped out with the skills required. She moved through several other tabs, with little joy again. They weren't making her search easy. Her next port of call would be the individual faculties.

A tap on the shoulder and the sound of a familiar voice interrupted her task. "Hiya."

Abby spun round in a seat to see Samantha Huxtable standing there with a mug of tea and a Rich Tea biscuit.

Abby smiled. "For me?"

Samantha laughed. "Oh, no, sorry. I thought I would just stop by. You know we were talking about that case I've been given?"

"Yes, yes. The missing animals. Have you found Doris's pussy?"

"Ha ha, funny. No, and I'm still saddled with the case. And another report came in just an hour ago. A black Labrador went missing a couple of days ago. Anyway, it looks like it's been found. Dead."

Abby's mouth downturned. "Ah, that's a shame. Bless it."

"That's not the half of it. It was found dissected in the woods in Stanmer Park." Her voice dropped to a whisper, and she leant forward. "It's heart and lungs were removed. Whoever is doing this is one real sicko."

"That's gross. I feel sick thinking about it."

"*You* feel sick? I'm just about to go down there and have a look. I don't suppose you fancy coming?"

Abby shook her head vehemently. "No chance. Besides, I've a ton of digging around to do." She thumbed at her PC screen. "Sounds like a case for the RSPCA now?"

"Yeah, I've already put a call in to them. They are going to meet me up there. Wish me luck."

Abby winked as Samantha strolled off.

She reflected on their conversation as she returned to her research. The abduction and mutilation of a pet was not only horrific but bore possible parallels with their current case.

Abby pulled out her phone and sent Samantha a text.

> Let me know how you get on.

13

Abby had managed to track down a lecturer at Sussex university who could help them with their enquiries. She'd passed the details to Scott before his visit to the address for Margaret, the childminder.

Costa Coffee on Western Road was the last place Scott expected to be meeting a university lecturer in African Studies. On campus, yes, surrounded by stacks of dusty books and an untidy desk. He had imagined the lecturer in a tweed jacket with glasses and a beard, sitting in an old, creaky leather captain's chair. Instead, he saw a man in his thirties, sitting in one corner, sipping a hot drink. The man did have a beard, but that was where the similarities ended. He wore faded jeans and an open-neck white shirt with a chest full of hair poking out from the top.

"Simon Young?"

Simon stood up, greeting Scott with a broad smile and a firm, enthusiastic handshake.

"Thanks for taking the time to see me. I know my colleague Abby contacted you."

"It's a pleasure to meet you, Detective Inspector. Your

colleague suggested that I may be able to assist you on a case?" He returned to his seat. "Can I get your drink?"

Scott declined Simon's offer. "Is this your usual place for a meeting?"

Simon grinned. "I guess that's what most people assume when they put university and lecturer in the same sentence. Well, this is as good a place as any to meet. Frankly, it's nice to get away from that overflowing desk and old books."

Scott smiled, understanding the sentiment. He loved escaping from the office and grabbing a corner in Munch, his favourite café. "We're working on a case where the body of a child has been discovered with some limbs missing. He's of South African descent, and we've been advised by our partner agencies that this case does bear the hallmarks of a potential ritual killing. It's not something my team has dealt with before, so we are running blind."

Simon narrowed his eyes and nodded. "May I ask what limbs were removed?"

"His arms and head...and his heart."

Simon nodded again and furrowed his brow. "Yes, I'd agree, it carries the indicators of being a potential ritual killing." He strummed his fingers on the armrest. "A South African child, the head, some limbs, the heart. So yes, it certainly could be."

"Can you shed some light on why people would do this?"

Simon cleared his throat and sat forward, resting his elbows on his knees. "It sounds like a muti killing. The term 'muti' finds its roots in the Zulu tribe and in the Zulu word for tree. Its use is widespread in many African languages. Muti has been used for, gosh, a long time as a slang term to refer to traditional Southern African medicine. I've studied this. I've been to South Africa a few times to study the tribal communities in greater detail. I guess you could say it's a fascination of mine."

Simon took a quick sip of his drink before continuing. "The thing is, Inspector, traditional African medicine makes use of many spiritually concocted medicines. They contain nothing more sinister than everyday items like botanical properties, minerals and zoological composed formulas. These *loosely* termed medicines have been used to treat everything from headaches, anxiety, organ disease and high blood pressure, to increasing sexual potency."

Scott nodded and took a few notes.

Simon continued, "In my opinion, muti killings are nothing more than murder and mutilation to harvest body parts, which can be added as ingredients to medicine. Let me be clear here, they are not human sacrifices, nor are they religious in nature, despite what's documented or said about muti. They'll have you believe that muti brings good luck, good health, and prosperity and that the gods are being served. The victims – and yes, they are victims as far as I'm concerned – are often young children. Most are killed for their soft tissue, so the eyelids, lips, scrota, and labia have been severed – as well as entire limbs in your case."

"So it's not magical or mystical in your view?"

Simon shook his head. "In the eyes of those who believe in it, there is an element of that. Sadly, the victims are alive during the mutilation, because their screams are supposed to enhance the medicinal power. It is believed that medicines made from these killings will increase one's ability to excel in business or politics, improve agriculture or protect against a war. The list is endless, Inspector."

Simon sat back in the chair.

Scott digested his comments and shook his head. "That's mind-blowing. Has muti been going on for some time?"

"I'm afraid so, Inspector. Though it is difficult to find precise statistics – and trust me, I've looked – the earliest documentation appears to be in the 1800s. You must understand, Inspector, that people believe in things for different reasons. We all do. Science has eliminated our reliance on deities, but people on the African and Asian Continents still feel the need for something spiritual. They want a tool to structure their lives and guide them."

Simon paused as Scott added more points in his notepad.

"A report from the United Nations found ritualistic killings across the African continent, including Nigeria, Zimbabwe and South Africa, with Nigeria recording the highest number of cases. But their report also found cases in India and Nepal. A few were also spread across the UK, France, and USA."

Scott sat back, surprised. "So are we seeing more of these outside the African continent due to migration and human trafficking?"

"I can only make a guess, but yes, I would say it's because we're experiencing a greater migrant flow between countries. Many are heading to safer Western countries because of political and military strife and catastrophic climatic change in their own. Whether they arrive here legally or illegally doesn't matter. Wherever they end up, the religion and beliefs come with them, too.

"In the context of your victim coming from South Africa, during the 1990s South Africa experienced significant polit-ical strife with the ending of apartheid. There's been huge unrest in the political, economic, and social landscape there. Things were supposed to have changed. Sadly, they haven't. I guess that's why we are finding more migrants escaping from that country."

Scott thanked Simon for his time and his offer of continued help.

The meeting had been informative: he'd walked away with a bundle of notes and a motive for the killing. Whilst this felt like progress, the enormity of the task ahead weighed on him. It wasn't uncommon for children arriving in the UK to not be registered. It made them harder to track and easier to disappear.

With a wall of silence from a hostile local community, and a small group of frightened and suspicious asylum seekers, this case would test him.

THE SEARCH for Margaret Eze led Scott to a small apartment in the tight streets behind Brighton station. She lived there with another woman who, according to Patrick, had been sheltering Margaret and allowing the childminder to look after children at her residence. The location didn't alarm Scott but the position did. Five floors up with a balcony that was no taller than chest height, the apartment posed a serious threat to the safety of children.

Sandra Bello was the owner of the apartment and had lived there for a little over two years. Scott knocked on the door and heard the faint sound of the TV from somewhere within the apartment, and a shuffle of footsteps. He waited a few moments before knocking again. The footsteps grew louder. Several locks unbolted before the door opened a few inches. A dark, short lady with unusually large eyes gave Scott a penetrating stare.

Scott held up his warrant card, saying, "I'm Detective Inspector Baker from Brighton CID. Are you Sandra Bello?"

The woman stared at Scott's ID card, her eyes flicking between Scott's face and his photo ID. She nodded. "What is this all about?" she asked in a heavy African accent.

"I'm looking for Margaret Eze. I believe she lives here?"

The woman neither confirmed nor denied it.

He asked again. "It's a private matter. I'm looking for Margaret Eze. Is she here?"

The woman shouted something in her own language.

Scott heard more shuffling from somewhere down the hallway. Another person appeared behind Sandra. The woman looked in her late forties and was dressed in a knee-length, brown and grey tweed skirt, white blouse, and a thigh-length cardigan. She wore a black and yellow head-wrap that Scott knew was a dhuku from the research he'd been conducting.

She lowered her gaze. "I'm Margaret Eze. I've been expecting you. I'm almost packed," she said in a soft, sorrowful tone.

"Sorry?" Scott asked.

"You've come to deport me, haven't you?"

Scott shook his head. "I'm afraid there's some confusion here. I'm not from the Immigration Department. I'm not here to deport you. I'm here because I'm investigating the death of a child that we believe to be Michael Chauke."

Margaret gasped and placed her hand on her chest. Her breathing intensified. "Oh my Lord, sweet Jesus..." Sandra placed an arm around the sobbing woman.

"May I come in to ask you a few questions?"

Both women nodded and led Scott into to the lounge – a small room, sparsely furnished. A grey three-seater settee and armchair took up a large portion of the room. A small TV sat in one corner. A black glass shelving unit stood to one side of the room, packed with pictures of what Scott presumed to be family, alongside pictures of village settings, mountains, and flowers.

Scott sat in the armchair while the two women sat together on the sofa. Sandra offered her friend several tissues as Margaret shielded her face with one hand. Tears escaped through the gaps in her fingers.

"What's happened?" Margaret muttered.

"That's what we're trying to determine. We believe that a

body discovered a few days ago is that of Michael. His parents have been informed, and we are waiting on confirmation of his identity."

Margaret looked up, puzzled. "But I have a picture of him if you want to know what he looks like. Have Anneke and Patrick not seen the body?"

"I'm afraid that's not possible. Until all forensic tests and the post-mortem are completed, it will not be possible for them to see it."

Crease lines appeared as Margaret frowned. Scott moved on before Margaret could question him further.

"I understand that you childmind here?" Scott glanced around the room. He noticed the lack of children's toys, books, and puzzles that would be expected at any childminders' residence. Perhaps they had been put away in another room. "How often did Michael come here?"

"Rarely. Maybe once a week, when Patrick and Anneke had other things to do."

"What was Michael like?"

The smallest of smiles brightened Margaret's face. She gazed off to the side. "He was a good boy. Kind, gentle, and very smart."

"Did he ever mention anything to suggest that he was in trouble or worried about something?"

Margaret shook her head. Her eyes narrowed, as if deep in thought.

Scott continued, "What about when Patrick and Anneke came to drop him off? Did you sense anything wrong with his parents?"

Margaret glanced at Sandra; Scott was sure they had exchanged unspoken words.

She faced Scott. "Patrick and Anneke never came here. They never dropped him off or picked him up."

Scott looked at the two women. "I don't understand."

"It was always Pastor Mabunda who would bring the children. He organised everything. He said he wanted to make it easier for everybody. He would bring them and take them back."

Scott frowned. "And he did that for all the children you looked after?"

Margaret nodded.

"So you never saw any of the parents?"

Margaret confirmed Scott's suspicions. "The pastor said he would take care of everything. He said he had the gift of God, and praise be the Lord, we trusted in him. He said the fewer people who knew where I lived, the less likely that someone would find me and send me back..."

Her head dropped, and she wrung her fingers in her lap. She was clearly scared, frightened, and unsure of her life and future.

14

The mid-afternoon sun carried some heat at this time of year. Dipped low in the sky, its bright brilliance cast long shadows across the office floor. The team perched on desks and chairs as they focused on the incident board. Raj passed around the chocolate fingers, which were quickly snapped up. Scott relayed the outcome of his meetings with Simon Young and Margaret Eze.

Simon's information attracted the most attention.

"So if this voodoo witch doctor stuff is so powerful, do you think we can get a potion to give Mike more success with women?" Raj teased.

The dig was met with laughter.

Mike nodded at the box of chocolate fingers Raj held. "I do just fine, mate. It's you who needs the help. What do they say? People unlucky in love often turn to food for comfort. I rest my case."

Helen stifled a laugh behind her hand.

Scott added with a wry smile, "Better still, maybe I'll get a potion made up that gets my team to take the job seriously." Even though he was teasing, the team refocused again. "With what I've heard from Simon and the NCA, our investigation has all the hallmarks of a ritual killing, and I think that has to be the focus of our investigation. I also believe the pastor is connected to our case. From those we've spoken to, he seems to carry a high degree of respect, but I feel that there's a measure of intimidation as well."

Scott turned to Helen. "Simon spoke about muti killings not being sacrificial or religious but carried out for medicinal or business purposes. But he also added that there have been more recent cases that have had the sacrificial element to them. I get the impression it's so ingrained in their culture that it is seen as normal or even expected."

"So where do we go from here, guv?" Helen asked.

Scott wasn't sure. He felt as if he were racing around in circles. With it being such an unusual case, the only way he saw to maintain the integrity of the investigation was to treat it like any other murder.

He turned towards the incident board and studied the information gathered so far. "We need a breakthrough with other families who are in a similar situation. I can understand why they are scared. Whether they've come here legally or illegally, they are looking for a better life. That's why I think we're meeting a wall of silence. They are suspicious of authority. In their home countries, the authorities are often corrupt and untrustworthy. And there's the added concern that they might be deported from the UK."

Scott took a moment to think back over his meeting with Simon.

"From what Simon mentioned, there's deep-rooted corruption in the police and judicial services. They take bribes and dish out their own violence. Extortion rackets are commonplace, men disappear, and women are sexually abused. I'm not surprised that they see all figures of authority in the same light."

"We can't all get tarred with the same brush, guv," Helen said.

Scott lifted one hand. "While I agree with you, I think it will take time to gain their trust, and time isn't something we have. Mike, I know you've contacted the community support groups and churches. I need you to push harder on that front. Take Helen or Abby with you and get your faces in front of them. I'm not being sexist here, but it's a very male-centric environment in their home countries. If you go with Helen or Abby, it might soften their view of us."

Mike nodded. "I'll get on to that right away, guv."

Scott continued, "As we know, officers in the Met had a similar case. I'm going to put a call in to them this afternoon and lean on their experience. Any snippets they can give us might help. In the meantime, Abby, get back on to the NCA and find out as much as you can on muti killings. There may have been other occurrences in different parts of the country. It's a long shot, but try the South African embassy. Perhaps they could put us in touch with the right intelligence services at their end?"

Abby confirmed the request and then moved on to her updates. "Forensics have confirmed the body is Michael Chauke. The buccal swab and blood confirmed a DNA profile match with his parents. We knew that anyway from the birthmark, but it's good to get valid confirmation."

"Can you inform his parents, please, Abby?"

"Yes, guv. There's also feedback on the blanket that Michael was wrapped in. It's an outdoor blanket commonly found in most camping stores. We're compiling a list of relevant stores in the Brighton area, and we'll contact them first. If we draw a blank, we'll look at shops outside of the area and online stores."

"Good call, Abby. Any further update on the PolSA team?" Scott asked, looking for feedback from someone.

Abby replied, "It's a blank there, guv. No body parts at all. No blood traces either. The other items recovered were not connected to our case. However, the claw hammer had DNA traces belonging to a suspect who's wanted for a string of burglaries, so uniform are taking that one. I looked at the sex offenders list, and nothing pops out. There's no one who displays such violent tendencies. Plenty of kiddie fiddlers, mind you, but there's no evidence of previous dismemberment."

Scott felt that might be the case. They were now following the muti killing line of enquiry.

"Do you remember Cara mentioning stomach content analysis?" Abby added.

Scott nodded as his mind tracked back to that conversation during the post-mortem.

"Well, other than the nuts and raisins, a white creamy substance found in his stomach was a ground corn mix. It's a staple food in Africa. They call it pap. He also had scraps of dried meat, springbok. I think it's like the meat jerky that the Americans eat."

Scott sighed. "Well, at least the poor boy was fed. How did you guys get on with searching the pastor's apartment?"

Raj sat up straighter and flicked through his notes. "Forensics have been over the place. There's no sign of blood anywhere. They lifted hair and fabric fibres. One of the hair fibres came back as a match for Michael, so we know he was in the apartment. Could all be legit? Whilst the pastor was there with us, he claimed that he held Sunday school for the children. If that's the case, it could account for the samples found. We've not identified any other child visitors so far, so we can't cross-reference."

Scott shook his head and grimaced. "I'm not so convinced, to be honest, Raj. The pastor seems to have had far too much involvement with Michael, even to the extent of taking him to the childminder's and bringing him back. Surely, that's a job for the parents? He doesn't give much away in his interviews. I get the impression that people are scared of him. Whether that's to do with the stuff he spouts as a pastor or something else, I'm not sure. But we have a child who's been murdered, and we can place the child in his apartment at some point. So either he's not telling us something, or he's hiding something. We need to dig up as much as we can about him."

The team agreed in unison. Some stared at their pads. Others stared at the grisly images of Michael on the incident board for a few moments before heading back to their desks and seeing out the end of their shifts.

15

Preparing dinner for their guests had proved a bigger challenge than Scott expected. Jonathon ate anything, but Abby was the difficult diner. She wasn't keen on fish, hated red meat, didn't eat meat on the bone and dreaded anything that had too much fat on it.

Cara had sighed while she and Scott flicked through dozens of recipes online, trying to find suitable meals to fit her demands. They'd decided on an Italian-themed night, with classic bruschetta, which Cara prepared, chicken cacciatore casserole for main, which Scott was in charge of, and a classic Italian tiramisu, which was chilling in the fridge.

"Do you think they'll like the food, Scottie?"

"I hope so. If Abby pulls a face or picks the food apart, don't panic. She does that with everything she eats."

Having finished the last of their preparations, Cara tidied up. As she brushed past Scott, he reached out and pulled her close and rested his hands on her hips. He breathed in her perfume and fixed his soft gaze on her.

"What?" Cara asked as she frowned.

"Nothing. You look stunning tonight."

"Well, I try. I want to create the right impression."

Scott smiled and kissed her. "You do. Trust me, you do. I'd like to skip the meal and have my dessert right now," he said, pulling her hips into his.

"Down, boy. You sure you put the brandy in the tiramisu and didn't drink it?"

The doorbell rang, giving Scott no time to reply.

"Show's on." He squeezed out from between Cara and the kitchen worktop.

Scott answered the door with Cara in tow. Abby introduced Jonathon to them. He was a tall man at six feet, about the same as Scott, clean-shaven with dark brown short hair, and green eyes. He was casually dressed in dark blue jeans and a white shirt that was untucked. He greeted Scott by shaking his hand, then kissed Cara on the cheek.

Scott wasn't too sure what he had expected of Abby's boyfriend. She had always preferred tall, well-built, rugged men. He was neither well-built nor skinny, more an average build with an exceptionally long neck. Jonathon towered over Abby's five-foot three frame.

Abby said she'd seen a survey of women in a magazine, and the results highlighted that height was the key to sexual attraction. Her summation was that men preferred to look down on a woman whilst women preferred to look up to men. Scott hadn't agreed with her assessment.

The conversation and wine flowed. Jonathon was easy to chat with. He joked, didn't take life too seriously, and even poked fun at himself. Abby appeared quieter than normal, nerves probably getting the better of her. Cara floated in and out of the room, fetching condiments, drinks, and playing her role of hostess to perfection, with Scott helping to serve the drinks.

Scott peppered Jonathon with many questions. "What plans have you got for the business?" "Does the business do well in the face of online competition?" "What do you want to get out of life?"

An unperturbed Jonathon replied honestly, seeming to enjoy the frank discussion.

Scott only pulled back when Cara squeezed his thigh, a sure sign that he'd crossed into interrogation mode.

But then Cara faced just as many questions from Jonathon. "How does it feel to cut open a body?" "Does the smell put you off?" "What made you choose such a profession?"

Scott cleared the plates away after the main meal and prepared the desserts whilst Cara found herself explaining the finer points of post-mortem procedures.

Abby followed Scott into the kitchen a few minutes later. She nudged Scott in the ribs. "Well, what do you think?"

There was a hint of anxiety on her face as her eyes probed Scott's reaction.

He replied, "You're serious about him, aren't you?"

Abby shrugged, but her face reddened with embarrassment. She wrapped her arms around her waist. "I guess."

"Well, I'm not your father. If he makes you happy, then I'm happy for you."

Abby threw her arms up in despair. "That's hardly a ringing endorsement, is it? The way you questioned him in there, anyone would have thought you *were* my father."

Had he come across as the overprotective father? Questioning his daughter's new boyfriend?

"Yeah, sorry about that." He wiped his hands and gave Abby a hug. "Listen, I've not said this before, but I care for you. You're my friend and colleague. And...I want to look out for you. I know you've had some bad relationships, and I don't want you getting hurt again."

At that moment, Cara came in holding an empty bottle of wine. She paused in the doorway. "Excuse me, Scottie, but she's already spoken for. Her boyfriend is in the other room, if you hadn't noticed?" She nodded in the direction of the dining room.

Scott and Abby laughed. "I'm just giving her a pep talk, love. She was worried about what I thought about him."

Cara waved him away and gave Abby a tight squeeze. "Don't you worry about what Scottie says. Jonathon is lovely. He seems kind, attentive, caring, and above all else, he can't stop talking about you in there."

Abby blushed as she hurriedly made her way back to the dining room.

"Did I sound like an inquisitive father?" Scott asked Cara, now doubting himself and feeling self-conscious.

"Hello, why do you think I squeezed your thigh? I was trying to tell you to shut up." Cara planted a soft, lingering kiss on Scott's lips.

She made a move to grope his groin. A whole bottle of red wine was making her horny.

Scott fended her off. "Enough, woman, you have an insatiable appetite."

"Spoilsport," she grumbled, picked up two plates of tiramisu and walked out.

Midnight had come and gone by the time Jonathon and Abby left. Jonathon had been just as chatty when they left as when they had arrived. It was past Abby's bedtime, and Scott could tell she had been flagging since ten p.m.

Pleased with how the evening had gone, Cara and Scott stumbled into bed after cleaning up. Scott continued to recount the success of the night without realising that Cara had fallen asleep moments after shutting her eyes.

16

In the chilly darkness, he parked the car and got out to listen. For company tonight he had a nocturnal audience. The owls hooted in the trees, and rodents scurried amongst the leaf litter on the floor of the forest.

He stepped around to the back of the vehicle and opened the boot. It took a few moments to unload everything before he set off, following a winding path amongst the woodland. Rows of trees shielded him on all sides, a thick blanket of darkness that crowded him. Carrying two bags and a crate of small plastic containers slowed him down. A slippery floor and exposed tree roots caused him to stumble like a drunk and drop his load.

He cursed, picked up his belongings and continued.

The track carried on upwards for some time. He slipped off to the right and ducked under several branches that were blocking his route. A hundred yards farther on, the tree line thinned, and he arrived at the small opening. A sliver of moonlight spilled through the sparse canopy, acting like a searchlight and offering him the first glimpse of his destination. Ahead were posts and a wire fence. The shed just beyond.

He paused. The chill licked his face and crept under his clothes, tightening his skin like the bitter seaside wind on a winter's day. His teeth chattered, and he pulled his thin coat tighter. After carrying his load for what felt like miles, he should have been hot and sweaty. Perhaps it was the anticipation chilling him rather than the cold.

After unlocking the door of the shed, he let himself in, glancing over his shoulder one last time for unwelcome visitors. He felt safe inside. Everything he lived for, he could experience here. He lit the circle of candles on the floor. The air was still except for the odd draught that crept through gaps in the walls.

The flames captivated him as they danced. They were steady and bright enough to relieve the darkness of the room but not strong enough to read under. The items around the candles cast shadows that stretched out, as hands on an old analogue clock would. The wicks blackened; the wax turned to liquid, running down the sides and onto the glass plates.

He unrolled his bag of instruments and selected a sharp craft knife, which he placed by a large shallow pan. The skull he'd placed outside the circle of candles smiled at him, its face illuminated in the soft light.

He chanted the words that he'd been taught by Xabi, his mentor.

"*Kwangathi lo mnikelo uletha ingcebo nenhlanhla.*"

He was sure that this offering would bring wealth and luck. He repeated the chant, increasing the tempo and preciseness of his words.

His eyes widened, his head spun, and his breath came short and fast. Picking up his sacrifice by its legs, he attached it to the A-frame that he had built. His hand trembled as he reached for the knife. He bit his lip and tightened his fingers around the handle; his fingertips turned white with the pressure. A shiver rattled him.

His sacrifice struggled and screamed, but only for a few moments before the craft knife cut a deep wound across its throat. Silence followed as the blood pulsed out, forming a pool in the shallow pan. Steam rose as a sickly-sweet smell filled the air.

He bowed and muttered, "*Kwangathi lo mnikelo uletha ingcebo nenhlanhla.*"

Supporting the head in one hand, he continued to carve through the neck until it separated from the body.

He needed to work fast. He couldn't keep the gods waiting. The offerings had to be warm.

He placed the severed head on a bed of feathers, then took the craft knife once again and sliced down the centre of the body.

A warmth touched his fingers as he reached in; the heat and blood wrapped his hands in the gloves of death. With the warm heart in one hand, he cut it out.

He cupped the heart in two hands and raised it above his head before closing his eyes.

"*Kwangathi lo mnikelo uletha ingcebo nenhlanhla,*" he shouted three times.

Euphoria spread through him uncontained, like a bush fire. The hairs on his arms prickled in excitement. He inhaled deeply, soaking up the magnetic energy that was circling him.

Pleased with his work, he smiled.

With his precious gift stored away until tomorrow, he padlocked the door.

A final look around confirmed he had not been followed, so he started his journey back to the vehicle.

17

C ara woke to the sound of Scott whistling a tune. She opened one eye, glanced at the clock and groaned.

He shouted, "Morning, beautiful!"

It felt like mere seconds ago that she'd collapsed in bed. She reached down and pulled the covers over her head. The music continued to play.

"Breakfast time!"

She peered out from under the covers to see Scott holding a glass of orange juice in one hand and a tray with toast and tea in the other.

Cara groaned. "What's this? National Let's Annoy Cara Day?"

Scott plonked the juice down on the bedside table and placed the tray on the bed. "No, it's room service, madam. You worked so hard yesterday, and last night you exhausted yourself. No doubt it was a real chore getting through a bottle of wine. I thought you might need a lie-in and then a pick-me-up."

From beneath the covers, Cara gave him a finger salute.

"That's not a nice way to greet your boyfriend," he replied, climbing over the bed and pulling the covers down. "Besides, we do have to get up. I'm due in at ten, and you said your first PM is at ten thirty a.m."

Cara groaned again. She hauled herself up in bed, rubbed her eyes, and ran a hand through her knotted hair. "Next time we do a dinner bash, we do it at the weekend, agreed?"

Scott smiled. "Next time we do a dinner bash, you don't drink so much, agreed?"

Cara playfully punched him on the arm.

"Oi, that's assault, you know."

She reached for her juice. "Does that mean you have to handcuff and frisk me now?"

"Frisk you?" Scott laughed. "You've been watching too many American cop shows."

A comfortable pause followed. Cara took a bite from her toast and sipped her tea. The ease with which they could sit in silence reflected just how far they had come as a couple, and how much they enjoyed being in each other's company.

Scott leant over and kissed her on the cheek. "It was good fun last night, wasn't it?"

Cara nodded. "What did you think of Jonathon?"

Scott raised a brow. "Actually, he's a really nice bloke. He dresses well; he likes to talk. A real conversationalist and genuine."

"You sound surprised?"

"Well...not so much surprised. I guess more pleased than anything. Abby's told me on many occasions how rubbish her old relationships were. Big drinkers, big smokers, verbally aggressive, and a complete mismatch in personalities. I think she'd got to the point where she'd lost faith in finding a truly meaningful relationship. Abby had become very sceptical. I think she held back on her feelings to protect herself, and that's why people found her cold and defensive. A defensive mechanism, if I'm honest."

"Thank you for that assessment, Dr Baker," Cara teased. She had learnt a little herself about Abby and agreed. "The main thing is that's she's happy. She looked terrified last night on the doorstep, and you didn't help by giving him an interrogation." Cara laughed.

"Well, I'm only looking out for her," he mumbled as he went off for a shower.

SCOTT HAD ONLY JUST ARRIVED at the office when Abby came searching for him. She was desperate to know his thoughts about Jonathon. Like a nervous teenager, both excited and petrified of receiving their A-level results, she eagerly awaited Scott's feedback.

He kept it complimentary, much to Abby's relief. He sensed that Abby was seeking confirmation from him that Jonathon was decent.

Abby followed by stressing just how much they had enjoyed the evening.

"On the journey home, Jonathon kept telling me how much he had enjoyed the evening. He said you and Cara make a lovely couple, and that we should return the offer of a meal. I agree –"

The conversation stopped abruptly when Scott's internal phone rang. He picked up. It was the desk sergeant. He listened with a stony face and scribbled down a few notes. Then he asked a few questions and replaced the handset.

"Problems?" Abby asked.

Scott sighed and stared at the ceiling. "We've just had a report come in. A five-year-old boy's gone missing."

"Coincidence?" Abby speculated.

"You know me; I don't believe in them. He's five years old, black, lives on the Whitehawk estate, and his family are asylum seekers."

Abby's eyes widened as she swore.

"Exactly." Scott threw his pen on the table, rose from his chair and grabbed his jacket. "What pisses me off is that he's been missing for three days, and his parents only reported it this morning. Dolores Carter is a care worker who works for a support group. The group has close contact with families seeking asylum. The parents told her, and she called it in."

———

DOLORES CARTER, a slim African woman with braided hair, answered the door. Scott noticed her exceptionally large silver earrings that dangled from her stretched earlobes. She showed the officers through to a small lounge where a couple sat huddled together, a look of fear in their eyes. Dolores introduced Scott and Abby to them and offered the pair a seat.

Scott took the lead in interviewing Sizani and Musa Buhari whilst Abby took notes.

"I'm Detective Inspector Baker, and this is my colleague Detective Sergeant Trent. Dolores called to inform us that your son, Nathi, has been missing for a few days. Can you tell me what happened?"

The parents glanced nervously at each other, both uncertain as to who should speak. Their hands were tightly woven for support. Musa, the boy's father, glanced at the officers.

In broken English he began, "Nathi, just a small boy. He said he wanted to play with other boys. We let him play in street. He used to playing out in our home country. He went out and not come back." Musa looked at his wife, who was sobbing heavily, her shoulders shaking with grief. He placed a reassuring arm around her shoulder and pulled her tight to his body.

Scott nodded sympathetically. "Do you know who he was playing with?"

"Just other boys," the father replied.

"Do you have their names, or know where they live?"

His question was met with silence. The parents exchanged more frightened glances before looking in Dolores's direction.

Dolores nodded. "I can provide you with their names later, but I've already been to their houses, and no one has seen anything. They said that one minute the little boy was playing with them, and the next he disappeared."

Scott took a picture of the boy from the parents. A small chubby face and a wide radiant smile stared back at him. He held his arms up aloft in some gesture of victory, clearly conveying a joyous moment. Sadness and apprehension ran through Scott as he contemplated just how frightened the young boy must be. He pushed away a dark thought. What if he had already taken his last breath?

Scott asked a few more questions before leaving.

"Doesn't sound good, hey?" Abby said, walking back to the car.

"No. Another child, another asylum family," Scott replied. "And missing three days. That's a pattern right there."

His phone rang. Mike's name appeared on-screen.

"Mike, what's up?" Scott put the call on car loudspeaker so they could both listen in.

"Guv, enquiries on Pastor Joseph Mabunda uncovered that he's travelled to the UK eleven times in the past two years and stays for six to eight weeks before returning to South Africa. He returned to the UK two weeks ago, a week prior to the discovery of Michael's body."

"Thanks, Mike. We're on our way back now."

18

In Scott's eyes, the timings were a little too close for them to be random. Information obtained from the South African embassy confirmed that on each occasion, the pastor had obtained a UK visitor visa. He had never stayed the maximum six months allowed under each visa. Scott assumed that if the pastor continued that trend, he would leave in less than six weeks. That time frame only heaped further pressure on Scott and his team to uncover any connection with him to Michael's death.

Scott checked Google and clicked through pages of websites that he'd pulled up on muti killings. The images horrified him. A common thread appeared in all the images: they were children, young children.

He winced as he read the information out loud. "Whilst being mutilated, it is believed that the noise from the agony of the victims strengthens the potency of the various soft tissues and organs being removed."

He glanced through several cases from South Africa. One article in 2009 reported how a ten-year-old child had been taken and was found in bushes near her home the next night with her internal organs removed. In another, the murder occurred in 2004, where a ten-year-old boy had been struck on the head with an object. The murderers had then chopped off his penis, his hand, and his ear.

Scott shook his head, a mixture of repulsion and fascination flooding through him. No matter how hard he tried to look away, the morbid allure of these cases pulled him back in.

Another case highlighted the murder of a six-year-old girl who had been found brutally mutilated. As he read each case, he hardened to the facts being presented. The little girl's tongue, heart, and intestines had been cut out of her whilst she was still alive. After she had died, the murderers had put her body in a plastic bag. Her body was found five days after she was reported missing, floating in a nearby river.

Scott sat back in his chair, his mouth agape.

Just when he thought he'd read it all, this female victim had experienced savagery beyond his comprehension.

He ran his hand through his hair in disbelief as he read the last few lines again. "The left hand had been severed, her tongue cut out, and there was an incision from her navel to the end of her buttocks. Her private parts had also been removed."

He'd seen enough.

Scott questioned how such killings could be allowed and, more to the point, accepted in some parts of the world. The fact that cases of muti killings appeared to be on the rise in the UK alarmed him even further.

The evidence, the cultural background of those involved, and nature of the crimes all pointed towards sacrificial or ritual killings. However, Scott couldn't rule out the possibility of this being a more straightforward case of abduction and murder disguised to look like muti.

Once again, he stared at his notepad. Pastor Mabunda's

name had a question mark next to it. Margaret, the childminder, had a *NO* written next to hers. Scott's gut told him that Margaret wasn't involved in the murder. She'd been more concerned with finding a way to stay in the country.

He added Nathi Buhari, the most recent child's name, to the page. When the boy's parents had informed Scott that Nathi in Zulu meant god is with us, the irony hadn't been lost on him.

With nothing more to go on, Scott needed to expand his search and learn more about the complexity of ritual killings. A call to Simon Young would be a good starting point. He'd also ask Abby to put the heat on Dolores Carter. The support worker had provided them a way into the secretive world of asylum seekers. Until her intervention, they'd met a wall of silence. The council had given them the locations of all the families, but none had been willing to talk. Many had even refused to answer the door when members of Scott's team had visited.

Scott headed over to the incident board and added a few more photos of Nathi. With one child murdered and another missing, there was a growing argument for a press appeal.

His thoughts were interrupted by Helen hanging up the phone and calling his name.

"Guv, we hit a positive match on the blanket that Michael was wrapped in. We found a couple of local camping, outdoor-type shops that stock this item. Two of the shops have recorded sales of the blanket in the last three weeks."

Scott looked at the incident board. He stared at the forensic pictures of a crumpled, red, bloodstained blanket. "Excellent work, Helen. Get down there. We need any CCTV footage of the transactions, and purchaser details. Take Abby with you."

Abby and Helen hurried through the station. As they neared the back entrance to the car park, Abby heard her name being called. Samantha Huxtable jogged up behind her.

"Is it urgent, Sam? We have to dash."

"No worries, I can catch up with you later. I'm heading out in a moment, too. But quickly, remember that sodding case I've been given?"

Abby nodded as she searched her bag for her car keys.

"Well, I've just had a report of a dismembered pooch being found. It had its heart removed."

19

Scott met Simon Young in his campus office after calling him. The lecturer rose from his worn swivel chair and shook Scott's hand.

"So, are you ready to become a fully paid-up witch doctor?" Simon's serious expression threw Scott for a moment, but then he smiled.

Scott returned the smile.

Simon pointed to a chair. "Please sit. How can I help? I sensed a pressing urgency in your voice when you called."

Scott sat and took out his notepad, ready to refer to some earlier notes.

"We're hitting a brick wall with this case, Simon. We have very little forensic evidence other than the blanket and sheeting that the boy was wrapped in. We have no witnesses, and the community and others connected to the case are proving less than helpful. What I need from you is help in tracking down the person responsible. Is there anything that you can tell me in terms of who or what we should be looking for?"

Simon rested his elbows on the table and formed a

steeple with his fingers. "When I liaised with the Investigative Psychology Unit of the South African Police Service as part of my study into muti, they estimated that fifty to three hundred lives are lost to ritual murders every year. It's widely practised, accepted, and feared. They don't have accurate figures because most murders are recorded simply as murders irrespective of motive and dismissed as the work of some crazy nutjobs."

Scott leant back in the chair. "I can't comprehend how there's no thorough investigations."

"You're not kidding. Despite South Africa being the most developed African economy, Inspector, a large proportion of its population still believe power, wealth, and health are better guaranteed by witch doctors than stockbrokers, market analysts, and medical doctors."

Scott nodded. Simon had opened up a world he never knew existed. The closest he'd come to this was watching Baron Samedi, the voodoo spirit of darkness and death, in the James Bond movie *Live and Let Die.*

Simon continued, "Muti has two purposes, either medicinal or for luck and power. What you need to determine is which one is the motivating factor for your case. Has anyone come over here seeking medical help, or are there African businessmen in Sussex looking to build or grow businesses?"

Scott shrugged, not knowing the answer to either suggestion. His mind wandered as he crunched the sizeable task ahead. He looked around Simon's room. Adorning the walls were various African tribal prints and a dark wooden tribal mask that appeared to be too thin and long to fit a face. A bookshelf in one corner held more books than it had been designed for; the majority Scott could see related to African culture and history.

Simon grabbed a lever arch folder from a shelf behind him. He flicked through it until he found what he needed.

"The fact is, Inspector, that people who want to do better, people who want to be promoted at work, gamblers and politicians who want to win and even bank robbers who seek to get away with crime turn to muti back at home."

"It has that much of an influence?" Scott asked, surprised.

Simon nodded and raised a brow. "The nature of what body parts have been dismembered plays a key role. How the body parts are used varies according to what one wants to achieve. So, for example, the victim's body parts – and sometimes the contents of the victim's skull – are used as ingredients for ridiculous and outrageous get-rich-quick concoctions that are eaten, drunk, or smeared over the ambitious person who's requested help."

"That's crazy!" He couldn't even fathom that rational human beings would consider these heinous acts to be effective.

"And it's not just kids. It's weird, Inspector. Various body parts are used for different purposes." Simon paused for a moment as he referred to some notes in his folder. "I know of one case where a man who had difficulty fathering children killed a father of several children and used the victim's genitals for muti purposes. In another case, a butcher slapped each of his products with a severed human hand every morning before opening his shop. Why? Because he saw it as a way of invoking the spirits to bring customers to his shop."

"So it could be someone trying to bring luck?" Scott asked.

Simon shrugged. "It's possible. It just so happens that children are targeted because it is believed that virgins hold greater power, and that magical powers are awakened by their scream as they meet their premature death." Simon paused for a moment. "I see it as symbolic logic. The idea is that another person's dick will cure one of impotence, or that a perpetrator's far-sightedness will be strengthened by gouging out and eating the victim's eyeballs. Even blood is thought to increase vitality, so they guzzle that down too."

"So our victim was beheaded and had his arms and heart removed. If we're working on what you suggested earlier, the head was removed in relation to someone's desire to be... ambitious, possibly?"

Simon glanced at his notes and agreed. "The heart may have been removed because it represents life and longevity. It's what gives people power. So again, someone wanting to dominate and be powerful may have asked for this ritual. The arms or hands can be buried under the door of a shop or business. It's believed that these items bring customers to the premises, making the owner wealthy."

"I see." But Scott didn't really see it at all. In all his years of being a detective, he thought he'd seen and heard it all. This leapfrogged over every other sadistic act he'd ever encountered.

"Of course, Inspector, we need to consider medicinal muti killings too. In Africa, particularly South Africa, medicine is manufactured using traditional means. And I use the term *traditional* loosely. Healers or witch doctors grind up human body parts and mix them with roots, herbs, seawater, and also use animal body parts to prepare potions and spells for their clients. The resulting medicine can be rubbed on the skin, into open wounds, or ingested as per the witch doctor's instructions. So you may wish to look into anyone from the community who's unwell."

A feeling of overwhelm crept into Scott's mind. There was so much to take in. He had gathered more than enough information and had certainly opened his mind as to motives for Michael's killing and the potential abduction of a second child.

"Just one final question, Simon. Do they have any special tools and instruments that they use?"

Simon shook his head. "Not particularly. They can use anything from sharp kitchen knives to machetes, shards of glass and even an axe. But there are other things that can be used as part of the ritual. Some are truly mind boggling. I do recall one particular case where the perpetrator had been arrested with what the police called a medical bag containing a woman's placenta, the severed head of a cat, and chicken skin. All paraphernalia that could be used as part of a ritual process."

20

Back in the shed, he prepared to hone his skills in front of his mentor, who sat silently in one corner. The past few weeks had allowed him to experiment and practise the exact techniques he'd been taught. Each opportunity had filled him with fascination, with excitement and ecstasy.

He took his time in placing each candle in a large circle. From the bag of chicken feathers, he placed two feathers at chosen intervals around the circle. Taking the large plastic tub from one corner, he lifted out one of his prized possessions: a dog's skull. He had enjoyed stripping the skin and flesh to reveal the white bone structure beneath. He placed it at the top end of the circle farthest away from him. Upon lighting each candle, the darkest corners of the shed glowed bright. Mystical shadows from the flames danced across the walls.

Finally, he emptied the crushed herbs from a smaller container and placed them to one side and unrolled his tool-kit. Gleaming steel blades reflected in the candlelight. He traced his forefinger along the flat edge of one knife. Beautifully crafted tools. Perfect killing machines that had the strength to cut through the thickest flesh, tendons, and cartilage. A large eighteen-inch machete felt heavy in his hand as he lifted it just a few inches to judge its balance.

He briefly glanced at the boy, who looked dazed and tired. He'd held him here for a few days. With just a blanket to sleep on, the boy had shivered in those moments of lucid awareness. Awake now, the effects of the medicine were wearing off. His eyes were dark and empty. He'd devoured the handful of nuts and raisins the man had given him upon his arrival.

He lifted the frail boy and placed him in the circle of flames. His small head bobbed from side to side. The first signs of fear showed in his wide eyes when the heat from the flames began to lick his body. The man stroked the boy's head and offered him the smallest of smiles for reassurance. Then he pushed the boy back onto the floor. The boy wriggled beneath the man's forearm on his chest that was pinning him to the ground.

Terror widened the boy's eyes. He screamed at the sight of the shimmering blade coming closer to his face. The boy's arms and legs flailed; his heels scraped across the floor.

His high-pitched, terrified screams echoed off the walls. His agony lasted a few brief seconds. Then the boy's eyes flickered close, and his throat gurgled.

"*Amandla avela empilweni entsha*," he chanted.

He had practised those words over and over to ensure that, when the time came, he would be able to say them without stuttering.

His mind swirled; his brow glistened. His heart pounded in his chest. As he sat back on his heels, he could hear his pulse beating in his ears.

Time was of the essence, and he needed to work fast now.

He severed the boy's head, then lifted it aloft with both

hands and chanted once again before storing it in a clear plastic container. Pushing that to one side, he worked on removing the other body parts as requested by his mentor.

Sweat from the man's brow dripped into his eyes. He blinked away the stinging sensation, aware he was being judged.

His mentor remained seated in a shadowy corner, observing his every move and every word. How he delivered this ceremony would determine whether he would be trusted to conduct one alone.

He glanced over his shoulder; a nod from Xabi confirmed that he had delivered what was expected.

Happy with the endorsement, he turned and continued his work.

21

Scott's gamble of applying pressure on Dolores Carter paid off. He arrived the next morning to find her sitting in the station reception with Sizani and Musa Buhari. The three were ushered into a private interview room, where they were joined by Abby, whilst they waited for Scott to arrive.

Scott came in armed with his notepad. Dolores was sitting to the left of Sizani, holding her hand. Musa sat to his wife's right, holding her other hand. He pulled out a chair to join Abby on the other side of the table and continued to observe the boy's parents. Fear and suspicion showed in their worried eyes. Sizani appeared to have been crying for some time, her eyes puffy and red. Musa sat tight-lipped, his jawbone tense, as nerves and frustration appeared to have taken hold.

The bland grey walls matched the sombre mood. Abby did the introductions for the benefit of the tape, introducing all those present and providing the caution.

Scott moved his attention from the parents to Dolores. She smiled softly.

"Dolores, I understand my colleague Abby spoke to you yesterday. As a result of the conversation, you've been able to find out some information that could help us with our investigation. Is that correct?"

Dolores nodded once. "I spoke to a few families last night. The majority are just too frightened to say anything. You have to understand something, Inspector. They are thousands of miles away from their homes. They've fled persecution, torture, famine, and war to make a better life for them and their children. It stands to reason that they are cautious of everyone. But Musa told me something yesterday that you need to hear." She turned towards Musa and gave him a nod.

Four pairs of eyes drilled into Musa. He licked his dry cracked lips as he slowly brought a cup of water up to them. He took a few sips. "I have valuable information for you. Please protect us."

Abby leant across the table and cupped her hands. "Protect you from who?"

Sizani glared at her husband, who raised his hand to pacify her.

"We don't want to be sent back. We like England. But he has our son."

Scott and Abby exchanged glances.

"Who?" Abby asked.

"The pastor."

Both officers stiffened. Abby motioned for Musa to continue.

His voice softened to a whisper. "Five boys and girls have been taken in just a few weeks. One of them was Michael. They are taken by the pastors as offerings to the gods. There are powerful African businessmen who have come to England, and the children are being offered to the gods in return for wealth and prosperity."

Scott looked down at his notes as he processed what Musa had told him and what he had heard from Simon Young. It was all making sense. "What is the name of the pastor?"

"Pastor Mabunda. He came to the country with another man called Pastor Xabi. We know Pastor Mabunda very well, but the other pastor we do not know. He is in Brighton. He is a very weird man. He has magical powers and very cold eyes. He can deliver what most people can't. No one challenges him. It is said that if you anger him, he can pull your heart out with his bare hands."

Musa made a fist to demonstrate.

"Have you seen him?" Scott asked.

Musa shook his head. "He came here about eight weeks ago, but he has not been seen for six weeks. No one sees him, just the businessmen. They pay him lots of money to make their wishes come true."

"Has Pastor Mabunda taken the children?"

Musa shook his head. "I don't think so. He's a very religious man. He was teaching all our children about God. But he also does not look Pastor Xabi in the eyes. No one does. Everyone is frightened of Xabi..."

Scott noted the fear in his eyes.

"Has Pastor Xabi taken the children, then?"

Musa nodded.

"And where can we find Pastor Xabi?"

Musa shook his head again. "I don't know. Please find our son. We want him back."

SCOTT AND ABBY burst through the doors and headed over to the incident board. The team gathered as Scott and Abby relayed the outcome of the interview. Scott added Xabi's name to the board. A nervous energy rippled through the team.

Scott said, "Our number one priority is to find Xabi. By all accounts, he's hardly seen and is feared by many in the community. They believe he possesses magical powers."

"Any clue to his whereabouts?" Helen asked.

Scott shook his head. "He's not been seen for six weeks. Start with the airports and ports. We need to know if he's left the country."

"And the missing four children? Any idea on where they're being held?" Helen said.

Scott shrugged. He didn't have the answer. "Abby, split the team into two. One team looks for Xabi, the other for the children. Ask around the churches and community centres. Also, check with the other asylum seekers, look everywhere. If Xabi is in Brighton, then I want him in a cell. Mike, pull in Mabunda. He knows this other pastor. We need to identify the connection between them. Mabunda may not be responsible for Michael's death, but he's implicated in it, I'm sure of that. Get on it."

The team split off, and a flurry of activity followed. Mike grabbed his jacket and weaved his way through the desks, heading off in search of Mabunda. Helen busied herself online searching for African-based businesses with interests in the UK and Sussex in particular.

Abby pulled up Google and typed in Xabi's name. After a moment she called him over.

"Guv, you need to see this."

Scott pulled a chair alongside Abby's desk and peered at the screen. The page Abby had clicked on showed a black man with shoulder-length, tight, scruffy dreads. His black robes were draped over one shoulder. Other than the robe, Xabi appeared to be wearing nothing else.

"Fucking hell..." Abby swore.

It wasn't what he wore that had caused her outburst but the facial and body scarring. The pastor had thick burns to most of his face and upper body.

Scott watched a video interview where Xabi spoke, and with authority. He openly and publicly dared any of his critics to challenge his beliefs. He praised his god for providing him with special powers that were needed by pastors from all walks of life.

The reporter panned the camera away from Xabi to dozens of top-of-the-range cars parked in the pastor's compound. He boasted how prominent business people and celebrated church founders sought his help.

Abby smirked. "Not short of cash, then."

Xabi boasted that consultations cost a minimum of four thousand dollars, which excluded the cost of the rituals. He then went into detail about his ritualistic processes, part of which incorporated slaughtering animals and then spilling the blood on his god.

Abby turned up the volume as Xabi continued to speak. "I'm a priest, a powerful one of course, and I use my powers to heal the sick, help people who want to travel abroad, help traders get better sales, and protect people from fraudsters. I disempower witches and wizards and aid people who have one problem or the other. Well known for the wonders I perform in this country, I receive people from all parts and even people from other countries."

He gestured at the camera, and it panned around.

"Look at that." Scott tapped the monitor.

Xabi gave the reporter a brief look around his shrine. The inner shrine housed statues of several gods. There were many shelves containing boxes of talcum powder and Holy Bibles. The room had a sinister look to it due to the several razor-sharp machetes hanging from wall hooks alongside a rifle. A table to one side of his shrine had over a dozen gold rings, wads of money, numerous padlocks, and calabashes on it.

Xabi grabbed one machete from the wall and waved it around.

"Profitable line of business," Scott noted.

Abby pulled air through her teeth. "He's either a brilliant con artist, crazed religious lunatic or complete psychopath... And he's on our patch."

"I can see why he instils fear in those he meets. It makes sense now why Musa appeared terrified at the mention of his name."

"The fact he's disappeared off the radar for six weeks worries me, guv. Do you think someone's sheltering him?"

Scott was about to reply when Raj hollered from across the floor.

"Guv, there's a Darren Bartlett from the Home Office on the line. Says he wants to speak to you."

Abby and Scott exchanged a look of surprise. Scott grabbed the nearest extension.

He introduced himself and listened with interest. Midway through the call, he shook his head. "This is a murder investigation, not fodder for you!"

A constable came through the doors and headed over to Abby. He whispered something in her ear and handed her a sheet of paper. Scott spotted the double take she gave the information.

Scott slammed the phone down and let out an almighty sigh. He looked up at the ceiling.

"What's happening?" When Scott didn't reply, she added, "Guv?"

"Darren Bartlett is from the Immigration Department at the Home Office. He made contact because he felt it was only right we were informed of their intention to deport many of the families with failed asylum claims, regardless of whether they're going through the appeals process or not."

Abby sank back in her chair.

"Apparently, there's a family claiming sanctuary against deportation back to Sierra Leone, but their claim has been turned down, along with several South African families. His team gave them notice last week."

"What do we do, guv?" Abby asked.

"I disagreed with their ethics. The Home Office wants us to bring them out into the open because the families keep disappearing. And to cap it all off, the Home Office confirmed that the decision is being supported by the local MP, Alistair Woodman."

"The last thing we need is to lose families that may be involved in our case. What if some of those to be deported are the ones with missing kids?"

"Exactly, Abby."

She waved the paper she'd been handed by the officer at Scott. "Well, our job just got a lot harder, guv. A member of the public just reported a body part has washed up on the shore by Palace Pier. It appears to be a child's left arm."

22

The location couldn't have been worse. Scott stood by his car and scanned the scene. Palace Pier attracted visitors all year round, with over ten thousand visitors a day during peak season. Towards the end of summer, tourists and locals continued to flock to the Victorian pier. Had the location been deliberate, or had the body part washed up on shore from another area?

He walked alongside the railings and looked down at the scene. "This is just what the press wants, a juicy story," he said to Abby. "A spectacle."

Flocks of onlookers crammed shoulder to shoulder leant over the railings of the pier. They had a bird's-eye view of the SOCOs in their white suits, foot covers, and masks. Scott watched as they bagged up the arm and conducted a detailed analysis of the stony beach. A large part of the beach had been cordoned off with blue and white police tape, and a line of officers walked side by side, scouring the beach for any other body parts or evidence.

Abby sighed. "Do you think it's from one of our victims?"

"What do *you* think?"

A limb popping up on shore didn't scream random event to him. A child's arm, dark-skinned, was too coincidental considering they had a child's torso and legs in the morgue. It was becoming a criminal game of connect the dots.

Scott had more than sarcasm. There was a tinge of something else. Anger. A lunatic was roaming the town, and he hadn't found him yet. But he would.

"Why not dump it in a bin or somewhere it couldn't be found?" Abby suggested.

"Maybe they wanted us to find it – unless it's unconnected and came from a different part of the coastline."

"I'll check with the control room for Sussex, but I'll also check with Hampshire and Kent control too."

"Quick as you can, please, Abby."

Helen and Raj had taken a statement from the Spanish couple who had discovered the limb tangled in some seaweed. Raj approached Scott, with Helen a few steps behind. At first, the couple had thought it was a plastic limb from a mannequin, but the true horror of their discovery had soon dawned on them when seagulls began plucking at the flesh. The woman's screams had soon attracted a crowd of curious bystanders and the attention of Palace Pier security guards.

Raj continued, "The limb was discovered a little under an hour ago, guv. As soon as the couple found it, the security team from the pier called it in. The couple were too shocked to do much. Thankfully, security contained the scene whilst waiting for the cavalry."

"Raj, can you look into the tide times? They will help to determine if the limb was carried and washed up, or dumped. Helen, the pier has CCTV, and there's a camera slap bang in front of the pier. Grab a copy for the last twenty-four hours from both. Chances are this limb only appeared in the last few hours or overnight."

Both officers left as quickly as they'd arrived.

Scott couldn't help but notice how surreal the situation was. Tourists were visiting one of the most iconic locations in Brighton. The September sun warmed his face. Seagulls screeched and squawked as they floated across the thin wispy cirrus sky before soaring towards the fluffy clouds. The familiar smell of greasy fish and chips soaked in vinegar wafted in the air. A forensic team was examining a body part discovered on the shoreline.

The wide-open public place only added to the curiosity and visible shock from those gathered.

From where Scott stood, he had a good view of the scene.

A SOCO joined him. He was a well-built man whom Scott had met on a few occasions. "Sir, we've recovered the limb and have conducted our preliminary search of the area. We are going to do a second sweep just to make sure. The sooner we can get it done, the sooner we can get away and restore some normality around here."

Scott nodded his agreement. "What's the condition of the limb?"

"It's been in the water for a few hours. There's evidence of damage to the flesh, more than likely caused by marine life, and some abrasions. I suspect they occurred because of scraping along the shoreline."

"Any idea of an approximate age?"

"Young. From the size, you're looking at somewhere between the ages of four and six, maybe seven. No older than that."

Scott thanked the SOCO. Until they did a DNA profile analysis, they wouldn't be able to confirm whether it belonged to Michael.

WITHIN MINUTES of returning to the office, Meadows marched into Scott's office. Scott's head snapped up at the sound of the man's plodding footsteps. He wondered if his superior had planted a tracking device in his phone. Either that, or he possessed some sixth sense.

Meadows stood by Scott's desk and crossed his arms. "Does the limb belong to the dead boy?"

Scott shrugged. "Possibly, sir. It matches the age and skin colour. We'll have to wait for forensics to confirm."

A concerned look twisted Meadows's face, his lips tightened, and his eyes narrowed. "The chief super had a call from CC Lennon. Lennon isn't happy. He's in a sticky spot. Alistair Woodman MP is giving him grief about our team having a run-in with the Home Office. Woodman thinks we're interfering with the Home Office operation to deport illegals."

"Why is the CC worried?"

Meadows gave a dismissive wave. "Woodman is a friend and acquaintance of the chief constable. They've met at several social functions, police, and local community events. I think the chief constable has met Woodman frequently in Parliament. Anyway, I think Woodman believes we are obstructing their operation and should be more cooperative."

Scott clenched his teeth. His body tensed. This appeared to be another example of political influence interfering with police neutrality. "No disrespect, sir, but we are not interfering. This is at a minimum a murder investigation, but more likely an abduction and ritualistic killing. That's far more important than deciding whether someone needs to stay or remain in this country."

"I hear what you're saying, Scott, but –"

"So we can't afford for them to wade in mob handed." Scott risked overstepping the mark with his interruption. "We have a very small, frightened community of asylum seekers. We believe they hold the key to helping us identify who is responsible for Michael's killing. We have a very strong lead now. More importantly, our go-between, Dolores Carter – a support worker – is only just gaining the trust of this community in order for us to interact with them. If the Home Office go in, it's game over."

Meadows stiffened and pulled his shoulders back. "Scott, I admire your passion, and I understand your reasoning for speaking up. But don't interrupt me again."

Scott looked down for a moment. "Sorry, sir, I didn't mean to. I just hate it when someone up there tries to pull our strings."

Meadows nodded once. As he turned, he said, "Just be careful, Scott. We don't want to piss anyone else off."

***

Whenever Scott felt frustrated or annoyed, he'd escape from the office and grab a coffee or something to eat. It was how he defused a tense situation and calmed his thoughts.

Once again, he sought sanctuary at Munch coffee shop with Abby. He sipped on a green tea whilst Abby sipped on her usual soya latte.

"So is Meadows telling us to back off?" Abby asked.

"No, I don't think so. Alistair Woodman is influential. It's just a case of people knocking on each other's doors. Barrett or Bartlett – or whoever the man from the Home Office was – is used to getting his own way. When I didn't roll over, he got pissed off."

Scott took another sip before continuing. "He moaned to someone above him, who moaned to someone else above *them*. Before you know it, the local MP is getting involved. The CC doesn't want extra grief like that, so passes it back down the chain."

They paused in their chat when the waitress arrived to

give Abby her Spanish omelette and Scott his hot New Yorker melt.

"So what are you going to do?" Abby asked.

Scott thought for a moment as he juggled a piping hot piece of sandwich in his mouth. The melted cheese lashed the roof of his mouth. "We carry on. I think we need to move on this. The last thing we want is someone trying to shut us down."

"The families?"

"I think we need to talk to them. We have to get through to them. We need them to open up. We can appeal to them, tell them that we don't want this happening to any other children from their families. It's the only way I can think to gain their trust."

cott and Abby had eaten only half of their lunch when the call came in. With its close proximity to the police station, the staff at Munch was used to the police darting out the door at a moment's notice.

Driving north, Scott weaved in and out of the traffic. Abby clung to the door handle with one hand and received information via her phone in the other. Helen was at the scene, coordinating it until Scott's arrival.

As Scott pulled up to the scene, organised chaos was how he would describe it. A wider, outer cordon had been set up with reams of tape weaving in and out of trees. SOCOs were in the process of unloading equipment from the back of their white scientific services vans. Uniformed officers were jumping out of a personnel carrier and donning overalls. Helen stood beside the scene guard – the tall and dark-skinned PC Oju on this occasion. He was an imposing presence over the large expanse of open ground that surrounded a wooded copse.

"What do we have, Helen?" Scott asked.

"Guv, we have bloodied clothes in the woods beyond.

They look like boy's clothes. Young by the look of it. Hidden under the clothes was a human hand."

"Who found it?"

"A female jogger. She was following a trail through the woods and saw a heap of clothes by the side of the path. She stopped, took a look and called the police. Her name's Abigail Porter, and we have her details. Uniform took a statement from her, and I've also spoken to her. She's had to leave because she needs to pick up her little one from the nursery. But I told her we may need to speak to her again."

"We'll take a look so we know what we're dealing with, and then leave forensics to do their initial assessment." Scott looked over Helen's shoulder at a large, black German shepherd being harnessed by its handler. "See you have the dogs in? Good call."

"Thanks, guv."

Scott, Abby, and Helen signed into the scene log before kitting up in white paper suits, foot covers, and blue gloves. Crunching leaves and snapping twigs punctured the tranquillity of the wooded copse as they made their way along a path mapped out by the SOCOs. They followed the line of police tape until the familiar sight of a white forensic tent came into view.

A SOCO was laying out the discovered clothing as Scott peered into the tent. From his position, he could see a sweatshirt with a *Transformers* logo on it, a vest, and a pair of grey joggers. They were stained dark red. A macabre image of a child's hand stopped him in his tracks.

"Well, that's a right hand, and the arm from the beach was a left. If it all belongs to the same victim, then we're missing the rest of the right arm," Abby remarked.

Forensics had their work cut out.

Scott walked around the area just as uniformed officers formed a line to begin a search of the ground. The shade of the wooded canopy had made the ambient temperature cooler, which had probably contributed to a slower decomposition of the appendage.

The heavy panting of the search dog and the handler's footsteps jolted Scott from his thoughts. "Where shall we start, guv?"

The SOCO held the sweatshirt still inside the clear evidence bag up to the dog's nose and allowed the K9 to have a sniff.

"Merlin, find," his handler encouraged.

The dog criss-crossed the scene, looking up momentarily before sticking his nose just centimetres from the earthy floor. Scott watched the dog backtrack, stop, sniff and then move on.

The action went from static to full speed in a blink of an eye. Merlin tugged on his extended lead and lurched forward. All the officers stayed silent while Merlin and PC James Appleby did their work. They followed to avoid contaminating the scent. About thirty yards ahead, both dog and handler stopped. PC Appleby raised his hand to alert the team and called his dog to heel.

Scott raced over, followed by Abby and Helen. The discovery left him speechless.

The headless body of a young black child lay on the ground. His body had been discarded like a sweet wrapper. A lame attempt had been made to cover the body with leaves and broken twigs.

A mixture of grief and frustration left the three officers silent. Scott nodded in the direction of PC Appleby to confirm that he could continue his search for any other items. The magnitude of the investigation had just escalated.

"Helen, can you inform Dr Hall that we need her here immediately?"

"Are you thinking what I'm thinking?" Abby said.

"Sizani and Musa's boy?" Scott nodded. "Likely, I would think. He's been missing a few days. Fits into the same age group. I dread to think of breaking the news to them."

Scott rubbed the back of his neck to relieve the tension. His head pounded; it felt like two sides of a vice were slamming into it. "Once we've had confirmation from Cara, I'll drive by with a FLO and tell them we found a body."

Despite the body being partially covered, Scott could make out the wounds that had been inflicted on the poor boy. Not only had both arms been removed, but there was a large gaping hole where his genitalia should have been. Scott closed his eyes and swallowed.

Abby shook her head in disbelief and shivered. "Dead bodies I can deal with, but dismembered bodies is something that I find physically sickening."

Nothing could prepare her, or any officer, for the sights they had to witness. The most violent of deaths, the most horrific of scenes were often laid bare for them to investigate. No human being should ever witness what they saw on a daily basis, and this crime scene ranked up there as one of the most heinous acts a human being could inflict upon another.

Scott turned to look back at Abby. "Are you okay?"

Abby waved away his question. She headed back out of the copse.

Matt, the crime scene manager, joined Scott. "You think you've seen it all, and then you see this." He shook his head.

"Tell me about it. Have your team found anything yet?"

"Nothing here. We have a leafy floor that's making analysis harder. The ground is dry, so the chances of finding any footsteps are slim. We're scanning the forest floor for any traces of blood, as well as fibres. I think the team will be here for a while now that we have two sites to examine. I'll get this area taped off and a second tent set up."

"Keep me informed of any developments."

Matt raised his hand in confirmation and wandered back to the first crime scene.

The discovery of a second dismembered body confirmed this crime was connected to Michael's, as both carried similar injuries. It also raised further questions for Scott. Who did the limb on the beach and the one found a short distance from here belong to? This body or Michael's?

As Scott headed back to his car, two thoughts crossed his mind. The Whitehawk estate was within walking distance, and the area that the children played in was no more than a few hundred yards away. The nature of their deaths, their backgrounds, and circumstances, no doubt in Scott's mind that they were victims of muti killings.

SCOTT HAD HARDLY PAUSED for breath before he was summoned to Meadows's office. He knocked louder than he needed; Meadows waved him in.

His stern face set the mood. "I heard about the second body. Do you think this is connected to the ongoing case?"

Scott nodded. "I'm certain, sir. Both boys were victims of muti killings. I think there is an urgent need for a public appeal. Mike's just pulled in one suspect who we believe may be an accessory to both murders. We're confident that we've identified a second suspect who may be involved. I believe a press appeal could help. I really do. We need more eyes looking for this character."

"Who is this second suspect?"

"Pastor Xabi. He came over around the same time as the first suspect, another pastor. But this Xabi character disappeared about six weeks ago and hasn't been seen since. The team checked, and we don't believe he's left the country. I reckon he's still here and perhaps being protected. From what we've seen so far, people are shit-scared of Xabi. And he's nothing more than a butcher back in his home country. He thrives on violence. He's a hate preacher and has been responsible for more deaths than we can imagine."

Meadows took a deep breath and tapped the end of his pen on the table. He stared at his desk, then occasionally glanced at Scott.

Scott pushed on. "This person has to be in the Sussex area and is more than likely in Brighton. Wouldn't it make sense to get a press appeal out there? It may bring him out into the open and cause him to make a move that leaves him exposed. My hope is that he is spotted by someone. Let the public be our eyes and ears?"

There was an uncomfortable pause. Meadows rose from his chair and walked over to his window. He stuffed his hands in his pockets, rocking back and forth on his heels, contemplating his options. He turned and nodded at Scott.

"Okay, you have it. We'll set up an appeal for tomorrow morning. I'll contact our press officer and get the ball rolling. But I need to warn you, Scott –" Meadows jabbed a finger at him "– it's a tinderbox on the Whitehawk estate. There are reports of racism – rocks being thrown at windows, and late-night intimidation of the minorities who live there. We need to be extra vigilant, make sure the racial tensions don't escalate."

"Agreed."

Meadows flicked his head in the direction of the door. "Go and see what this first pastor has to say and let me know."

24

P astor Mabunda was sitting stony-faced as Mike and Scott entered interview room one. He showed neither fear nor dread. The officers took their seats opposite him. They'd waited until a duty solicitor was available.

A female legal representative sat perched on the edge of her chair, her fingers entwined and resting on the desk. Scott guessed she wasn't older than her late twenties. She exuded keenness and had an energy that was missing from the older, more experienced solicitors. It was likely the profession, the rules, regulations, complexity of cases, and long hours eventually took their toll.

Scott opened the interview after spending a few minutes sifting through his paperwork. It was a psychological tactic he liked to use to rattle the suspect. He'd built up the style using years of policing experience and exploring human patterns of behaviour. The psychological manipulation began before he even opened his mouth.

The physical layout of an interview room was designed to maximise a suspect's discomfort and remove their power from the moment he or she stepped inside the room. Four chairs, a desk, a CCTV camera mounted on the ceiling and bare walls. The lacklustre room created a feeling of unfamiliarity and isolation, which usually heightened the suspect's "get me out of here" reaction.

Scott began. "Pastor Mabunda, we're investigating the disappearance of another young boy, Nathi Buhari. Have you seen him?"

Mike and Scott had agreed prior to entering the room not to divulge their discovery of another body.

Mabunda glanced at his solicitor, who gave him the smallest of nods. "No."

"But you know of him?"

"Of course," he said, nodding once. "He came to my Sunday school."

"So you can confirm that Nathi has been in your apartment?"

"Yes."

"Once or many times?" Scott probed.

"Many times. Over a few months."

Mike leant back in his chair and took notes. His large stomach stretched his shirt buttons.

Scott cut straight to the point. "Where is Pastor Xabi?"

Mabunda's eyes flickered for a moment; he looked up to the left before narrowing his eyes, to regard Scott suspiciously.

"I don't know."

Liar.

"You see, we have information to suggest that you and Xabi have been exploiting your positions, to gain the trust of the families and their children. What do you say to that?"

Mabunda checked with his solicitor once again, who shook her head. "No comment."

"Do you know what muti killings are, Pastor Mabunda?" Scott asked.

"No comment."

"Here's my theory. I believe that you gained the trust of young children, used the Sunday school as a front to build that trust, and then introduced them to Xabi. We have four children still missing, one dead, and I believe that you're an accessory to the abduction and murder of Michael Chauke. What do you say in reply to that?"

Mabunda stiffened this time but refused to budge on his pre-rehearsed answers. Scott's questions around muti, Michael's death, child offerings, and Xabi's whereabouts were met with several "No comments."

Without further evidence, Mabunda couldn't be held in custody. He was released pending further investigation.

"Where do we go from here, guv?" Mike asked as they headed back to CID. "We have DNA to prove that the kids were in his apartment. But the Buharis are unwilling to make a formal statement, so even if Mabunda is an accessory to the abduction and murder of Michael, the evidence will not stand up in court."

"We keep digging, Mike. We keep digging. Someone will slip up if we keep applying pressure. Mabunda knows we're watching him, and if he knows where Xabi is, he'll try to warn him. That might flush Xabi out into the open."

THE TEAM GATHERED around the incident board. Following the release of Mabunda, the team shifted focus to identifying the whereabouts of Xabi. With a press appeal scheduled for tomorrow morning, hopes were high that the hunt for Xabi would be expedited.

"Guv, forensics came back following further analysis of

Michael's blood. They found..." Raj stumbled over the scientific name of the compound identified. "*Griffonia simplicifolia.*"

Scott circled his hand to speed up the feedback.

Raj read the formal findings. "*Griffonia simplicifolia* is a climbing shrub that grows in West Africa and Central Africa. It's a source of the compound 5-HTP, which works with the calming, anxiety-reducing neurotransmitter serotonin and the sleep-inducing hormone melatonin. The seed pods from the shrub are sometimes made into a supplement and used as a natural sleep aid."

"So can we assume that this compound was used to sedate Michael?" Scott asked, adding the information to the incident board.

"Sounds like it, guv."

Raj continued, "Abby and I went over to the Whitehawk, in what turned out to be a futile attempt to get some of the families to talk to us. Some wouldn't open their doors, and others just shook their heads and played dumb. They are either too terrified of us or Xabi."

"Or both," Mike offered.

Scott had to agree. As far as the families believed, everyone was out to get them.

Mike continued, "I did more digging around with community groups and churches. A while back, the families all met at a small community hall. It might be worth exploring, guv? The support group worker I spoke to said that a pastor used to run the group. Then the group just stopped meeting about seven weeks ago."

"Do you have contact details for the community hall, Mike?"

Mike handed him a slip of paper with all the details on it.

"Abby and I will pay the hall a visit," Scott said. "In the meantime, Helen, what's happening with your review of the CCTV footage near the pier?"

"I'm looking at it, guv, so is the Brighton CCTV control room. But it's like looking for a needle in a haystack. It's so busy. Locals, tourists, children's parties on a day out. It's just a sea of people. We're narrowing down the time slot, hoping to find something."

"See if you can nab a uniform or two to help you. We need images of any likely suspects now," Scott pressed.

25

W hitecross community hall was on the northernmost boundary of the Whitehawk estate. Buried amid a small complex of nondescript brown council blocks, it was dwarfed by its eight- and nine-storey neighbours. Built over ten years ago, the council had offered it as a focal point for the local community. It had seen its fair share of weddings, birthday parties, community meetings, and wakes.

The caretaker and council had endeavoured to keep the place clean and tidy, but the remoteness of the hall and its proximity to its neighbours meant that it saw more activity at night than during the day. The caretaker would do his morning round, a litter picker in one hand and a black bin bag in the other. Discarded beer cans, Rizla papers, silver laughing gas canisters, and needles were picked up every morning.

"Surely, if you put in a community hall somewhere, you put it in the middle of the community, not the bloody outskirts," Abby said in bewilderment as she stepped out of the car. "Who would want to traipse all this way on a winter's night when it gets dark by five o'clock?"

Scott agreed. It might explain why the hall was turning into a ghost town. With youths on bicycles and mopeds robbing and attacking the elderly for the few pounds they carried, it was enough to make most people avoid venturing this far.

They were there to see Barry Johnson, the forty-nine-year-old caretaker who had spoken to Mike. As they approached the front of the building, Scott found a man sweeping away dust and debris.

"Barry Johnson?" Scott asked.

The man stopped and held his broom by his side. About five feet seven inches tall, Johnson's navy, tight polo shirt stretched over his protruding belly. Faded, ill-fitting jeans hung low on his waist, exposing the top of his rear. The man bore several days of untidy stubble.

He looked like the type of man who enjoyed going down to the pub most nights for several pints and a packet of crisps.

"Yes, that's me," he replied in a rough, gritty voice. He licked his lips as he eyed the two officers.

"I'm Detective Inspector Baker, and this is my colleague Detective Sergeant Trent. We are from Brighton CID." They presented their warrant cards. "We wanted to ask you a few questions about a community group that used to hold meetings here. In particular, asylum seekers housed in the community. What can you tell us about it?"

Johnson scratched his head and narrowed his eyes, as if trying to recall. "That's right. There used to be a regular once-a-week thing where a load of those asylum seekers would turn up. They used to sit and chat for hours. Occasionally, you would get a member of the council turning up to answer questions they had. They all spoke a funny language, so I didn't have a clue what they were on about."

"Was there any bother here, trouble of any sorts?" Scott asked.

Johnson shook his head. "No, not really. Lots of tears, mind you. You'd always get at least one woman every week moaning and crying. It wasn't even crying. Screaming would be a better way of describing it."

The noise from a passing bus drowned out Scott's next question.

He repeated himself. "Did they organise these meetings themselves, or did someone else organise them?"

"No. It was organised by some priest bloke. He was the one who called and confirmed the booking each week. He'd be here to chat to them all. They would bring their kids, and the little brats would just be running riot."

Scott pulled his shoulders back to relieve a niggling ache in his back.

"And did this priest bloke have a name?"

The question caused Johnson to look away and frown. His lips moved as if he was talking to himself. His gaze sharpened. "Mab, Maby...or something like that."

Scott and Abby exchanged a glance. "You can't be more precise than that?" he asked.

Abby held out a picture. "Have you seen this man before?"

Johnson stabbed the picture several times with his index finger. "That's the fella. Maby something."

"You told my colleague that the meeting group was shut down. Why did that happen?"

Johnson rubbed his stubbly chin, the sound it made rasping in the air. "Well, it ended suddenly, if you know what I mean. One minute it was on, and the next minute I get a call saying that the community group wasn't allowed to meet here anymore."

Scott pursed his lips. "Who was the call from?"

Johnson shrugged his shoulders. "I can't remember; it was a while ago. All I remember was that it was a posh bloke calling from the council to say that the group wasn't allowed to meet there. The meetings had to end with immediate effect. He went on to say that failure to comply would mean that the community hall would be shut down. So who am I to argue? It's owned by the council, anyway. I just do what they say."

26

The darkness of the woods enveloped him, offering him protection from the outside world. On this occasion, he had parked the vehicle some distance away and had approached the dense woodland from a different direction. He knew that repeating the same patterns would attract attention.

Under the dark cover of night, he blended in. Cloud cover that evening assisted him with his mission. Without the brightness of the moon, he could move unnoticed between the trees. He stopped occasionally and listened out. He needed to be sure that he wasn't being followed. Despite the darkness, his familiarity with this route allowed him to move swiftly. The occasional rustling of leaves caused him to stop and wait before carrying on.

The path twisted and turned, leading him through corridors of trees that disappeared into the gloom and brought him to a familiar bend. He darted to his right, dipping under low-hanging branches, careful to avoid leaving any trace of his visit. The track opened out into a clearing. The familiar outline of the wire fence posts came into view. He paused by the edge and waited.

He didn't rush, convinced he could take his time. Once sure he hadn't been followed, he proceeded towards the shed.

The padlock clicked loudly enough to be heard some distance away. Once inside, he lit a small candle in one corner to provide some illumination. He had travelled light with just his roll of tools.

The little girl, dazed, weak and scared, cowered in the corner.

One by one, he lit the usual circle of candles. As each one glowed bright, the colour of the room was warmed by a reassuring orange luminosity. The still air provided the ideal environment for the flames. They stayed steady and were bright enough to relieve the darkness of the room. The teardrops of brilliant gold light mesmerised him. It was magical, mystical, and empowering.

He scattered flowers and the bundled herbs within the sacred circle before proceeding to open a Tupperware box. Having removed the chicken's claw and cat's foot, he placed them either side of his sacrificial bowl. He glanced around to ensure he had set out everything the way he had been taught by his mentor, Xabi. The instructions were precise, the demands specific.

Rolling out his tool bag, he'd already decided that an eight-inch, sharp, steel knife with a razor-tip point would suit the purpose today.

With the A-frame in position, he grabbed the girl and dragged her across the floor. He ignored her cries and strung her up by the legs. He pulled on the rope until she swung. The squeaking sound of the pulley was barely audible over her screams echoing through the shed. With the knife, he slipped the point in as deep as he could at the neck, cutting the jugular. The silence was restored as she bled out, her life extinguished in an instant. She'd suffer little pain.

"*Amandla avela empilweni entsha,*" he recited, euphoria coursing through his veins. His heart pounded like a bass drum in his chest.

His next task was to fillet her. After making a precise cut, the innards slid out and landed with a plopping sound on the floor. The warmth of the body cavity warmed his hand. The hot, sticky matter clung to his skin, making it hard to grab the heart. Each time he tried, it would slip from his fingers.

Several attempts later, he held her small red heart in the palm of his hand. He marvelled at its structure and its potency for life. The most precious gift to offer the gods.

Within thirty minutes, he'd sacrificed and gutted her. He breathed a sigh of relief as he stood. They would be pleased with the result. He was sure of that as he cleaned up.

With the girl dismembered and stored away in containers, he stepped out into the cold night air. He inhaled, and the chill penetrated the deepest corners of his lungs. Chills raced down his spine as the adrenaline wore off. He'd connected with the spirits tonight and offered the gods a gift, in return for good fortune and wealth.

Disappearing into the darkness, he decided to return soon.

27

As he raced into work, Scott decided the morning couldn't have gone better. Helen had worked through most of the night. Despite drawing a blank with the CCTV footage near Palace Pier, she had managed to get a hit on the purchasers of the red camping blankets. Two shoppers had used debit cards, a John Casey and a Daniel Johnson. Helen had already dispatched officers to the house of John Casey to enquire about his purchase.

The second shopper raised Helen's interest following further investigations. She had identified that he shared the same residential details as Barry Johnson, the caretaker that Scott and Abby had visited yesterday. Daniel turned out to be Barry's son.

Scott burst through the doors of the incident room. Helen and Abby were sharing Helen's PC and examining further details.

"A credible lead?" Scott asked as he took off his jacket and tossed it on the nearest desk.

Helen debriefed him. "Cotswold, an outdoor camping store on Western Road, sold two of the blankets in the last few weeks. Unfortunately, they only keep CCTV for a week. They didn't have video footage, but they could provide me with the transaction details. I'm still waiting to pull out more on the individual, but eighteen months ago he received two cautions from us with the RSPCA, for cruelty to animals."

Helen paused for a moment whilst she reviewed details on her screen. "In particular, he was cautioned for shooting birds with an air rifle. He kicked a cat and was found in possession of a large penknife. Neighbours complained of a smell emanating from Johnson's back garden. When the police arrived, they found evidence of blood. Daniel claimed it was from two cats fighting. Unfortunately, they didn't have any evidence to prosecute."

Abby added, "I know uniform are looking into the case of cruelty to animals and animal abduction, so I will pass this on to the officer in question, as I reckon they're linked to our case."

"It's time we had a chat with Johnson Junior," Scott said.

He grabbed his jacket and headed out the door, with Abby hot on his heels.

JOHNSON'S HOUSE appeared empty as Scott and Abby milled around it. With it being a terraced house, they were unable to go around the back. They found Barry Johnson at the community hall, preparing to open up. The caretaker stood up as they approached.

"Mr Johnson, do you have a son by the name of Daniel Johnson, aged nineteen?"

The man eyed them suspiciously. He nodded. "I do. What's he done wrong now?"

"We are just following up a line of enquiry. We understand he made a purchase from Cotswold on Western Road. A camping blanket."

"More than likely."

"And where is Daniel?"

Johnson shrugged. "Your guess is as good as mine. He's always out camping. Away every few days. He likes prepping, you see."

Scott furrowed his brow. "Prepping?"

Johnson cleared mucus from his throat. "It's, like, huge in America. Prepping means preparations, I guess. It's about preparing for a possible disaster or emergency by stockpiling food, supplies, ammunition, and all that stuff. People who do prepping like to think they can survive."

Johnson grimaced before continuing.

"Some even go camping for weeks to see if they can survive off the land. You know, all that bollocks about hunting, fishing, and surviving on the basics. He was telling me that prepping is a way of life, and there is always something new to learn, different tasks to do, and gear to purchase. He bought the blanket for camping out somewhere."

"Has he been doing this long?"

Johnson shrugged. "A good few years. To be honest, he went off the rails after his mum left. One minute she was here; next minute she upped and left. She snuck out one night, taking all the money from Daniel's money box and a load of her clothes and buggered off."

"And you don't know where she went?" Abby asked.

"Nah. There were rumours down at the pub that she met some fella and went off with him – good riddance. I think all this camping stuff was his way of dealing with it. He just withdrew. He didn't wanna talk to anyone, didn't wanna see anyone, and he's hardly spoken to me much since. He just does his own thing."

"And where does he do this camping thing?"

"Anywhere where there is open land forest. Ashdown Forest, Sussex Downs, anywhere where he won't get disturbed."

BARRY JOHNSON WAS MORE than happy to show them Daniel's room. He led the pair down a dark hallway in the small and untidy property. Scott could see the lounge to his left and the kitchen to his right. He glimpsed opened cereal packets, the contents spread across the worktop, a sink with dirty dishes, and a half-eaten sandwich on a plate. The distinct smell of tobacco hung in the air. Evidence of smoking was all around them. The once white ceilings were tinged a golden yellow.

Barry Johnson stood outside one door and nodded his head. "This is Daniel's room."

Scott glanced at the door that had a padlock attached to a large, galvanised steel hasp and staple. He looked back at Abby, who at this point looked bored.

"Does he always have this locked?" Scott asked.

Johnson shrugged. "Pretty much as long as I can remember." Before Scott could ask, he added, "And no, I don't have a key."

"We need to gain entry. Do we have your permission to break the lock and enter?"

"Well, as long as you explain it to him later."

Abby took a step back to give Scott more space. He shoulder-charged the door. Despite being fastened, the door offered little resistance. It broke from the hinges, sending the padlock scuttling across the floor. Scott asked Johnson to wait in the hallway as he entered, followed by Abby.

Abby and Scott snapped on blue latex gloves before touching anything. The dark, musty room hadn't been aired in many weeks. The blinds had been drawn across the windows, creating a stifling atmosphere. Every square inch of wall was adorned with posters and drawings of the occult. Many had images, signs, and symbols that Scott wasn't familiar with but had seen in his most recent research.

Shadowy black figures in dark robes were scattered amongst the images. Some were artistic in appearance; others bordered on sinister. Pictures of skulls painted on human faces caught his eye just before Abby beckoned him over.

On a bookshelf above the bed were books of the occult. Abby pointed to one titled *The Encyclopaedia of the Occult* and then another titled *The Occult, Witchcraft, and Magic*.

"Not your average reading that you pick up from the library, guv?"

Something caught Scott's attention out of the corner of his eye. He nudged Abby.

He looked closer at the white apron hanging from a hook on the back of the door. It looked more like a butcher's apron. The front was marked with trails of red and finger smudges. Another object he noticed was a small, white fridge no more than two feet high, tucked behind the door. A plastic tray sat on top with a selection of small craft knives, picks, and tweezers.

Abby took a sharp intake of breath as she stepped closer to the fridge. She knelt down and opened the fridge door. Light filled the dark room. A waft of chilled air accompanied the action. Scott saw various small Tupperware containers stuffed on its shelves.

Abby lifted one container; the contents swished and lapped up the sides. She peeled back the lid and looked inside.

"Shit, guv..." She looked over her shoulder at Scott. "It's a heart, for crying out loud."

"Put everything back exactly as you found it," Scott ordered. He stepped forward and glanced into the fridge. If his suspicions were correct, there wouldn't be a need to look in the other containers.

Scott straightened up. "Mr Johnson, does anything in this room belong to you?"

Johnson shook his head. "I've not been in here for years. Jesus..." He glanced past Scott's shoulder into the darkened room.

Scott showed him a key chain with three small keys on it that he'd found. "Do you know what these keys open?"

Johnson peered at them and shook his head.

"Mr Johnson, we have found some items that interest us. I will be organising a SOCO to conduct further investigations. For the time being this room is off-limits."

"Why?"

When Scott refused to elaborate, the man sighed and wandered off towards the lounge.

Scott and Abby left not long after the arrival of the SOCO. With a photo of Daniel in his possession, Scott needed to get it to the press appeal asap.

28

Hushed conversations travelled around the conference room. With a bank of cameras already trained on the stage, Scott and Abby joined Detective Superintendent Meadows as he prepared his notes. The room seated twenty-five people. There was at least the same number standing at the back.

Scott recognised a few familiar faces that turned up for every press conference. He nodded to the reporter and photographer from the *Argus* newspaper. He had spoken to the female reporter Tracey Collins frequently and had found her charming and professional. Not once had he been on the receiving end of a grilling from Miss Collins. Her questions had been probing but never loaded. She had sincerity and authenticity when conducting her questioning.

Meadows welcomed everyone and introduced Abby and Scott. He explained that Scott was the SIO in the case and would be happy to answer questions towards the end. Meadows began by explaining the circumstances around the first death before moving on to the second victim. He spoke about both boys coming from families seeking asylum. He fended off questions about whether the murders were connected.

One reporter, a large gentleman obscured in the back row, dragged his heavy frame up from the chair and asked if the murders were racially motivated. His well-worn, light blue shirt carried a sweat patch that ran down the centre of his back. He pointed out that sources on the estate claimed that tension had been building between the asylum seekers and locals for some time. Incidents of tit-for-tat assaults had left many residents fearful.

Scott interrupted him to highlight that because the case was ongoing, they were not in a position to either confirm or deny racial motives.

The reporter continued to goad the officers, his chest puffed out. He claimed he had knowledge of police chiefs taking a decision to not prioritise reports of racial attacks on the Whitehawk. He volleyed several accusations at the top table that silenced the gathered press.

"Why are the police not doing more about these attacks?" He sat down.

Keen to diffuse the tension and bring the appeal back on track, Meadows continued by explaining there appeared to be a ritualistic element to the murders, and they weren't just random killings. He emphasised this point when two other reporters expressed their concerns of a real risk of causing widespread panic amongst parents, in particular on the Whitehawk estate. As Meadows reassured them and the wider public that police had stepped up their patrols on the Whitehawk estate, the reporters nodded and made notes. Meadows looked straight down the barrel of the nearest camera as he said their main concern was the safety of the public.

The disfigured face of Pastor Xabi flashed up on the projector screen behind the three officers. A mumbled chatter rippled through the audience, as well as a few gasps. Flashbulbs lit up the room as photographers captured the grotesque image of Xabi.

Meadows gave Scott the nod to continue.

"We are particularly keen to speak to this gentleman, Pastor Xabi. He's from South Africa and arrived here about eight weeks ago. He hasn't been seen for the past six weeks, but we believe that he is still in the country and possibly still in Brighton. We are keen on any information relating to his whereabouts. We need the public to be our eyes and ears." Scott paused a moment, allowing those in the room time to commit Xabi's face to memory.

"Is he your main suspect?" came a voice from somewhere within the crowd.

Scott had to tread carefully. He didn't want to add further fuel to the fire. "We believe he has information that will be of benefit to us in this enquiry."

"Yes, but is he your main suspect? Is he responsible for the killings?" came the voice again.

"Not at the moment. We are following several active lines of enquiry and speaking to several people in relation to this case. This individual hasn't been found." Scott paused as he scanned the audience. "If any member of the public sees him, we would ask them to call the incident hotline number, which is on the screen behind us."

Tracey Collins in the front row raised her hand. "Considering Brighton is synonymous with child murders, and probably will be for many years to come, how do you think the latest killings will affect the community and the reputation of Brighton?"

Miss Collins's question touched a sore nerve with her fellow hacks. The 1986 *Babes in the Wood* murders was a constant reminder to Brightonians of a dark period in their history.

All three officers exchanged uneasy glances. Nobody looked sure of how to reply.

Scott thought hard before he leant into his microphone.

"Any crime where the child is a victim is always difficult. I'm sure you'll all agree, the taking of a young life ranks up there as one of the worst things that can happen in society. But what I can say is that we are using every available resource to find those responsible."

A lump formed in his throat. He swallowed it back. "Many of us in this room are parents, or have been parents, and we will do anything to protect our children. This ongoing investigation is no different. We will do everything we can to protect every citizen of Brighton regardless of their age, and bring those who commit crimes to justice."

Abby, sitting in the audience, gave Scott the slightest of sympathetic smiles.

Scott handled most of the additional questions.

Much to his relief, Meadows concluded the press appeal not long after.

THE TEAM GATHERED around the incident board, having watched Scott and Abby on the TV.

"That tosser gave you a right hard time, guv." Mike huffed. "I think he's from some right-wing activist newspaper."

"If he is, then that explains why he went off on one." Scott took a hefty glug of water to quench his thirst. He briefed the others regarding the discovery at the Johnson property.

"Do you think this Daniel is connected to our cases, guv?" Helen asked.

"We can't rule him out, that's for sure. We found containers filled with small organs and limbs. The limbs belong to animals. There were chicken claws, what looked like rolls of skin, eyeballs – you name it. And that's just what's been discovered so far. Once SOCO is done, uniform is going to turn the room over. We'll have to wait for analysis to confirm the origins of some of those organs."

Abby continued, "It's safe to assume that Daniel was dissecting and dismembering animals, but there could be human traces of blood, too. The SOCO found traces of blood on one wall that appeared to have been cleaned away."

"And the dad knew nothing of this?" Raj asked.

"He claims he knew nothing," Scott said. "We'll look at his background anyway."

A uniformed colleague entered the office and waved a few sheets of paper as he approached.

"Guv, we managed to identify one character from the CCTV footage by the pier. The images are low quality and grainy, but they show the same individual returning to the pier on several occasions and standing in the same spot, looking over the railings. He doesn't engage with anyone, doesn't look around, just stares at the water below. He's dressed odd, guv. Take a look."

Scott flicked through the sheets. A man with a long, black coat and black baseball cap appeared in all the stills. A flicker of excitement caused Scott's heart to thud in his chest. He stared at the figure one last time before handing the sheets to Abby, who passed them around.

Abby took a second glance, unsure if her eyes were deceiving her. "You thinking what I'm thinking, guv?"

Scott nodded. "It's not a great still, but he does bear some resemblance to Daniel Johnson. Look at the date and time stamp on pictures four and five. In picture four he's carrying a Sainsbury's bag, but in picture five he's not carrying anything."

"And the pictures are only ten minutes apart."

"So whatever he had, he disposed of it in the space of ten minutes," Raj speculated.

Scott agreed. "Even more reason to find him. I think he has a few questions to answer. What else have we got?"

Mike flicked through his notes. "I contacted Dolores. There's no sign of the missing and elusive Pastor Xabi. No one claims to know his whereabouts, and even if they did, she believes that there's still too much fear to speak. Most of the asylum seekers believe the pastor is a witch doctor and that he has incredible powers. Powers that allow him to cast spells from a distance if someone crosses him. Now, whether you choose to believe that bullshit or not, it's enough to frighten the living daylights out of these people. And keep them quiet."

Scott scratched his forehead and paced in front of the board. They now had a manhunt for two suspects. Both appeared to be experts in remaining covert and undetected.

"We need to find Daniel Johnson." Scott tapped the name on the incident board. "How is a different matter altogether. He's not been seen for two days now. That's not unusual because, according to his dad, he can go on one of his survival forages for up to two weeks."

"Needle and haystack springs to mind, guv," Raj said.

Scott turned to Mike. "You're the best man for this. Back in your army days, you survived on rations, stayed undetected, and lived rough. Do you have any thoughts on where we should start looking for him?"

Mike stood up and walked over to a large map of Sussex pinned to the back wall of the office. He traced his finger across the paper. "The problem is, guv, from Winchester in the West to Eastbourne in East, we're hemmed in by the South Downs National Park. You have a landscape covering over 1,600 square kilometres of farmland, ancient woodland,

and lowland heaths, plus all the villages and towns. As Raj said, needle and haystack."

Scott had to agree, but there had to be a way to narrow down their search. "I know, but if you were in his shoes, what would you do to avoid being detected?"

Mike stared hard at the map and blew out his cheeks. "I'd stay away from centres of population and the main roads. I'd stay close to streams where I could get water to purify into drinking water, catch fish for food, and carry out basic personal hygiene. Ideally, a stream close to a dense area of woodland that would provide shelter or material for shelter."

Scott nodded, impressed by Mike's assessment. "Great. Can you look into that? I also suggest we look at his phone records and see if we can get a triangulation on the last time his phone was used. He may be using a compass feature on his phone – in which case it has to be on – or some mapping feature."

Mike nodded and made some notes. "Shall I check to see if his car reg has pinged up on an ANPR anywhere?"

"Yep. If it has in the last forty-eight hours, then at least it'll give us his travel direction, to help us narrow our search."

Abby took a call whilst Scott talked to Mike. She waved her phone at Scott. "Guv, it's the super."

The team quietened and hurried about their to-do list.

Scott took the call.

"Sir?" He listened in disbelief as Meadows gave him an update.

Scott punched the desk. "I apologise for my language, sir, but they're taking the piss." He ran a hand through his hair in frustration. "They know we're in the middle of a murder investigation, right? And they didn't think to inform us first?"

Meadows spoke more before hanging up.

Scott hooked his hands behind his head and sighed. All eyes were on him.

"Guv?" Abby queried.

"The Home Office just raided the Whitehawk estate and arrested six families seeking asylum. According to them, they have failed the asylum process and are being moved to a detention centre near Gatwick airport."

Abby rolled her eyes; the others exchanged glances of frustration and surprise.

Scott added, "They've been on our patch conducting surveillance for the last few weeks without telling us. We knew nothing about it. Even the super just found out."

Abby looked livid. "Surely, they can't just stroll into town without informing us and leave us to pick up the pieces?"

"They can, Abby. The Home Office swoop was supported by the local MP, Alistair Woodman. No doubt he thought it was good for his reputation and a way of showing his support for the local community."

Scott's mind turned cartwheels. He needed to break this case. He couldn't comprehend what those two boys had gone through in their final moments of life. He needed to find justice for them because they deserved it. A major plank in his enquiry had just been removed.

The screw had tightened, and Scott felt it as his stomach churned. Alistair Woodman needed a visit. Scott asked one of his team to call ahead to arrange their impromptu visit.

29

"You *do* know we are going to get in a lot of shit for this," Abby remarked as they drove to Alistair Woodman's residence.

Scott stared at the way ahead. "I know. That's why I gave you the option to stay back at the station. If the shit hits the fan, I didn't want you going down with me. I need answers from Woodman."

"You're all heart, guv."

"Besides, Alistair Woodman MP has been in contact with the Home Office. If we can appeal to his better side, he may be able to reverse the Home Office's decision. The last thing we need is to scare the very same people whose help we need. The Home Office has really screwed things up for us."

Alistair Woodman appeared to have his finger in every pie. He enjoyed a degree of celebrity status in Brighton. Wherever there was a social event where dignitaries were invited, Alistair Woodman was there. With connections that appeared to extend beyond Brighton, the man had significant clout. And it was that leverage Scott hoped to use.

Woodman lived in Ovingdean, a small village to the east

of Brighton. It was close to the larger coastal village of Rottingdean about a mile away but retained its exclusivity. Scott had had a brief opportunity to investigate Woodman prior to setting off.

After announcing themselves at the intercom, Scott drove in through the set of electric gates of the address and cruised up the long gravel drive to the front of the property.

"Bloody hell," Abby exclaimed as a Tudor manor house came into view.

The Oving, as Woodman's residence was known, dated back to the seventeenth century, with additions added later. It had been described as one of the oldest residences in Brighton. The sheer splendour of the property likely left those who visited in awe. The north side, which was the original entrance, represented the oldest part, with flint walls and stone quoins, similar to those of the church close by. Over the years the house had seen many architectural changes.

According to what Scott had read online about the history of the house, the Oving had servants' quarters and a cellar. The most noticeable change was the addition of the southwest Georgian facade, which now contained the main entrance to the house.

"Didn't I tell you Woodman was born into aristocracy?" Scott said as they stepped out of the car and admired the grounds. "This pile has been in his family for generations."

Abby shook her head. "This isn't a house. It's a flipping mansion, or an estate, or whatever the toffs call it. It must be worth a bomb."

Scott agreed. "It's been valued at about three million pounds."

The setting couldn't have been more opulent, set in a beautiful walled garden on a plot of three-quarters of an acre. To the front, the formal garden was arranged in six rectangular beds enclosed by box hedging, and each with a central clipped yew surrounded by flowering shrubs and roses.

Scott spotted a four-car garage.

"This is crazy," Abby muttered as they approached the front door. There wasn't an inch of brickwork visible beneath the creeping ivy covering it in dark green leaf. "It makes the walls look like something out of the 'secret garden' in a child's book."

Scott knocked on the door. It was a few moments before someone answered.

A small, thin black man acknowledged them. He wore a black suit and white shirt. Scott put him at around his mid-forties, but he could have been older. He looked tired and weary and made little effort to maintain eye contact. He appeared nervous, agitated, and scared.

Scott held out his ID and introduced Abby and himself.

"We are here to see Mr Woodman."

The man stood to one side and looked at the floor as both Scott and Abby walked in. After closing the door behind them, the gentleman led the way. His footsteps were light, soft, and measured. His arms stayed still by his sides, a trait that Scott found unusual. When most people walked, they swayed their arms.

They followed the man through a large opulent hallway. Large paintings adorned the walls, and an intricate red, tiled Edwardian floor added depth and character. Most of the doors they passed were closed, but Scott spotted one room that appeared to be a large games room.

Scott slowed and did a double take when he saw a skull and horns of an animal above the fireplace. Scott couldn't identify the species, but the mounted remains resembled that of a wildebeest. A large snooker table sat in the middle of the room. No expense had been spared here.

The man waved him and Abby into a room that looked

like one of several reception rooms. The look in the eyes of the man who had greeted them concerned Scott. He appeared frightened, perhaps even nervous. The man gave one solitary bow of his head and took a step back just as a smartly dressed Alistair Woodman breezed in. Woodman's gaze bored into the black man, who glanced at the police officers and exited the room.

Woodman was a tall thin man, with a long face. He wore a dark grey suit, white shirt, and patterned tie. Round, thin, metal-rimmed glasses adorned his face. His dark brown hair had strong accents of grey on the sides. He strode towards Scott and Abby, extending a hand. Scott and Abby introduced themselves to him before he asked them to take a seat.

"How can I help you, Inspector, Sergeant?" he asked with stiffness in his voice. "If it's to attend any events, then please contact my press secretary. Although a simple phone call from your superiors would have been enough to confirm my availability for any such event."

Woodman's voice was stiff and upper-crust British, the type of strong British accent that came from years of boarding school, Oxbridge, and mixing in high society.

"Mr Woodman, we're here about an investigation. The murder of two young boys on the Whitehawk estate."

Woodman frowned, and his eyes narrowed. He pulled his shoulders back. "Yes, very unfortunate. Such a tragic sequence of events. Please do let me know if there's anything I can help you with, although I'm not entirely sure what that would be."

"Well, I hope that you can help. You see, we're striving to gain the trust of the local asylum community on the estate. We believe that they could help us with our investigation and build a picture of those who may have been involved in the murder of these two boys."

Woodman nodded. His steely eyes locked on to Scott's.

Scott continued, "The Home Office executed a raid, and I hasten to add, without our knowledge or consent. They removed six families to a detention centre. I believe that has seriously damaged the relationship we were trying to build with that community. And I wondered if you could get them to reverse their decision, just until we've completed our murder investigation, or at least smooth the way for us so that we can maintain a dialogue with those families."

Woodman cleared his throat and crossed one leg over another in a rather flamboyant style. "I'm not sure that would be helpful to your investigation. I saw your press conference yesterday, and you seem to have identified someone you believe is a suspect. So surely it makes sense to exhaust that line of enquiry first?"

"He's certainly a man of interest to us. And someone we'd like to speak to. But we believe that those families are too frightened to speak, so having them holed up in a detention centre will not help our case."

"Inspector, I have no jurisdiction over a Home Office decision. Yes, it's unfortunate that they carried out a surveillance operation without your prior knowledge. They have a job to do just as much as you. They need to remove those who have no entitlement to be in this country. We already have enough pressure on our social services. These families could have obtained asylum in several countries on the European continent prior to arriving in the UK. By sending them back, they will now have that opportunity to apply through the official channels in any of those countries."

"Mr Woodman, I don't think it's as simple as that. I'm not here to judge whether they have a legal entitlement to be here or not. My job is to investigate a double murder. But surely those who are escaping persecution, war, drought, or famine deserve to be protected?"

Woodman shook his head. "That may be, Inspector, but

my job is not to represent them. My job, and one I was duly elected to do, is to represent the people of Brighton. Now you know, and I know, that the Whitehawk estate has experienced its fair share of publicity, with crime, unemployment, poor social housing – and the list goes on. The local community takes a very dim view of people who sponge off our state. Economic migrants have no right to be in this country. I am voicing the concerns of my constituency. It doesn't matter whether the migrants are African, Syrian, Ugandan, Eritrean, or any other nationality, the view remains the same."

Scott sat tight-lipped.

Woodman adjusted his glasses. "Off the record, as you know, the Whitehawk estate is predominantly a white community. There is tension between my white constituents and a very small immigrant population that is scattered across the estate."

Scott clenched his jaw as he listened to the man's twisted mentality. Racism took many forms, but Scott found it abhorrent that a Member of Parliament was displaying a clear contempt for those who had suffered misfortune.

Scott raised his voice in frustration. "Mr Woodman, you're entitled to an opinion, but once again I'm not here to discuss race, nor a person's entitlement to be here. I'm investigating a series of murders. All I'm asking from you is that you discuss a possible reversal or delay of the deportation process with the Home Office until after we've completed this investigation."

Woodman's face shuddered with anger. "Inspector, we're going round and round in bloody circles. I have no influence over the Home Office, nor do I wish to interfere with one of their investigations. I strongly suggest that if it concerns you that much, you raise it with the chief constable."

"And that's it?" Scott tried his hardest to remain calm. Sweat prickled his back; his pulse throbbed in his temples.

Woodman stood. "Inspector, Sergeant, I think I've been more than courteous in allowing you to come into my home. But you've now outstayed your welcome. My butler, Stephen, will show you out." He shouted, "Stephen! Step–"

The same man who had greeted them at the door appeared in the doorway before Woodman had even finished calling his name.

"Ah, there you are. The police are leaving now, so show them out. Good day to you both. If you have any further questions, then please contact my press secretary, Priscilla Matthew-Jones."

With that parting comment, he turned and left through another door. His rapid footsteps reverberated down the stone corridor, accompanied by mutterings.

"That went well," Abby said. She puffed out her cheeks.

Scott rolled his eyes. "I thought so, too."

SCOTT HAD RUFFLED A FEW FEATHERS. Within minutes of arriving back in the office, he was summoned to Meadows's office. His gamble of getting help from Woodman had backfired.

"What on earth possessed you to go see him?" Meadows fumed. He paced around his room while glaring at Scott. "The chief constable wasn't happy to receive a call from Alistair Woodman. Within minutes of you leaving, Woodman was on the phone to CC Lennon bending his ear about harassment, unethical behaviour, and a waste of police time."

Scott couldn't help but laugh. "Unethical behaviour? The man is a racist. I merely went there to see if he could use his influence in trying to delay the Home Office's decision to deport the families. Those families could help us to unlock the reasons behind these murders and flush out Xabi. They are frightened individuals. We're doing whatever we can to gain their trust. And the Home Office rode roughshod over all of us."

"That may be, Scott, but the man has clout. Everyone up there has clout." Meadows pointed at the ceiling. "I don't particularly enjoy getting a call from the chief constable asking me why my officers are interfering with Home Office protocols."

"Sir, I'm trying to run a murder investigation – a *double* murder investigation. If we had known that the Home Office was about to do a raid, we could have at least asked them to hold off for a few days, or even a few weeks until we had closed this case."

"Scott, it will not happen. You, me, or anyone else in the station cannot overturn a Home Office decision. We can't go around asking for favours from MPs. Make do with what you have, and don't go knocking on Woodman's door again. Clear?"

Scott conceded on this occasion. He could see both Meadows and Lennon were in a difficult position. Nevertheless, it continued to annoy him that his job was impeded by the handcuffs of political influence.

30

W oodman sat in his plush study, contemplating his next step. He glanced over his shoulder to make sure that he was alone before dialling the number. It rang for what felt like an age. He hung up and dialled again, cursing under his breath. "Answer the phone."

On the second try he got through. "Listen, we need to speed things along. There are too many people snooping around. And frankly, someone in my position can't afford for that to happen. Do I make myself clear?"

A hoarse voice replied, "You seem to forget exactly how beneficial this relationship is to you. I'm sure a man in your position can influence things in a way that, shall we say, takes the pressure off you? You're a well-connected man."

"I don't need the unnecessary attention. Sort it."

"Don't worry, my friend. We are nearly finished. The final processes are taking place now. As far as I am concerned, it is business as usual. But I need something in return."

"What? I'm already sticking my neck on the line for you. It's all right for you because you'll be gone soon. But I need to cover my tracks."

"I need your assurances that you will protect me. I, too, don't want the attention of your authorities. I need safe passage out of this country after it is done."

Woodman sighed as he listened to the man's demands. "You'll have safe passage; I'll organise it now. All the channels will be open. You'll be gone before they even realise. After, I suggest we slow this operation down, find a new avenue into this country –"

The line went dead.

31

F eeling tired and hungry, Scott left Abby as the acting SIO for the evening. He'd had enough. It had been all go since returning from his holiday, so he took the opportunity when Abby suggested that he knock off early.

Scott turned up at the mortuary to take Cara out for dinner. He sat in her office, clearing some emails from the job phone whilst she finished writing up the results from her final post-mortem of the day. She furiously tapped away on the keyboard, keen to complete her paperwork and make the most of her evening with her man.

They arrived at the House Restaurant in the Lanes, regarded by many Brightonians as their best-kept secret. The outside impressed Scott the most. It was a converted, double-fronted Victorian residence with plenty of aged character and charm. The moment they walked in, he felt as if he'd walked into someone's home dining room. Despite being set over two floors with dining areas dispersed off a central staircase, it still had the feel of a lived-in residence.

"Well, I must say this is a lovely surprise, babes," Cara said as they perused the menu.

The smell of food wafted around them. Cutlery rattled on plates, glasses clinked, and the din of conversations melted into the background.

Scott couldn't take his eyes off Cara as she enthusiastically scanned the menu. Despite being dressed in her work clothes, she looked great. Grace, elegance, sophistication, and sultriness were words that sprang to mind when he looked at her. Her dark hair flowed in curls over her shoulders and down her front. She was a beautiful woman, and he never tired of looking at her.

She looked up and caught his eye. "What?"

Scott smiled lovingly and shook his head. "Nothing. I could just look at you for hours."

"Ah, bless you, Scottie. You must be blind. I'm just little old me."

He reached out and placed his hand on hers. "You're more than that. I do love you."

"And I love you, Scottie, but enough of the slushy stuff. I'm starving." She gave him a playful wink.

"You're always starving," he teased.

Cara paused for a moment and studied Scott's face. "You look tired and stressed. We could have easily had a night in and a microwave meal tonight."

Scott sighed and blew out his cheeks. "I am stressed. It's been a tough few days. Of all the cases that we could have dealt with, we're dealing with the murder of two young boys – and in the most awful way. I won't lie to you; the images of those boys are stuck in my head. I can't begin to imagine what their lives were like before, and what they went through at the end. I would love to say that they didn't suffer, but from what I've discovered, they experienced something much worse."

Cara gave Scott's hand a reassuring squeeze. "I know, babes. If I'm honest, it's affected me too. But thinking about it isn't going to make you feel any better. You need to catch who did this; it's the least you can do for them. Listen, you've taken the night off. You need a break. Let's try to park work to one side and just focus on us."

Scott heard the truth in her wise words. Anyone in their positions needed to switch off and feel normal like most of the diners sitting around them.

Cara ordered the wild mushroom risotto, and Scott the fillet steak.

"Spain seems like a long time ago, doesn't it?" Cara asked as she poured her second glass of wine.

"It does. It's almost as if we never went." He chuckled.

"What's so funny?"

"I was thinking about that day we hired a car and drove to Ronda in the mountains. The road had so many tight bends and sheer drops that you felt ill. We had to pull up so that I could take over the driving. I just remember you sitting in the passenger seat with your eyes shut and head tilted back, thinking that you would throw up any minute."

Cara crossed her arms in mock annoyance. "Well, I suffer from car sickness, and it couldn't get much worse up there."

"And then when we were in Ronda, you peered over that bridge and looked down at the one-hundred-and-twenty-metre drop to the bottom of the gorge and nearly fainted." Scott burst out laughing.

Cara shook her head. "Ha ha, very funny. I'm glad to see that taking the piss out of me amuses you so much. That's blown your chances tonight if you thought you'd get some."

Scott tried his hardest to stifle his laughter.

They spent the best part of three hours at the restaurant, relaxing and enjoying each other's company. They ripped through two bottles of wine, enjoyed their meals, shared a few jokes with the waiters, and they had been normal.

Swaying as she came out into the fresh salty air, Cara

grabbed hold of Scott's arm. She buried her face in his neck and whispered, "Thank you for such a lovely evening."

32

An early morning run had been just what Scott needed to dust the cobwebs off from the night before. He had left Cara asleep in bed while he ran down to the seafront to meet Abby. He rarely had time to share moments like this with his friend. Both of their diaries were hectic.

Even though the pair worked shift patterns, they rarely stuck to them. A ten p.m. finish would often roll through to midnight, especially if they had a prisoner in and needed to get the case to CPS. Such irregularities in their working hours would throw their personal and social lives into chaos.

Scott felt sorry for Abby. Adam and Sophie, her children, were often cared for by grandparents. As much as she wanted to be home more often, the pressures and perils of being a single parent meant she couldn't give them the time and energy they deserved. However, neither child seemed to mind.

Sophie, who was fifteen going on eighteen, spent most of her evenings holed up in her bedroom, exchanging messages online. Because of her age, more and more of the messages were focused on the hot topic of boys. She was taking more of an interest in make-up, spending an inordinate amount of time on her nails, shaping her eyebrows, and experimenting with different looks – sure signs that she was fast approaching adulthood.

Abby's little boy, Adam, approaching twelve, did what most boys of his age did. He spent every waking minute on his Xbox, oblivious to anyone else in the house. Adam only ventured out of his room to grab a can of Coke and a bar of chocolate or a few biscuits before retreating to his sanctuary.

Moments like this when Scott and Abby went running together really helped to cement their friendship. It was more of a serious run for Abby and a jog for Scott. He would do most of the talking. Abby, on the other hand, would push her body hard against the clock. She was a masochist.

Abby used the opportunity to update Scott on the overnight developments, which by the sounds of it, wasn't much. She added that she had left by ten, leaving Helen to follow up on some potential leads before she clocked off at midnight. Whilst she had Scott alone, she quizzed him on his night out with Cara.

A semi-darkness cloaked the seafront as they pounded the pavement. Early morning commuter traffic was weaving its way past the grand facades of famous hotels. They passed the impressive, white, Victorian frontage of the Grand hotel, synonymous with Brighton, on their left. A landmark known to all, it had stood there for over one hundred and fifty years. The hotel was illuminated like a large Christmas decoration beneath large spotlights that cast a multitude of light and dark shadows across the front.

There wasn't a better place to run, in Scott's opinion. With the buzz of Brighton to his left and the calm and tranquillity of the sea to his right, the location could only be surpassed by the scenic trails through the Sussex Downs.

They ran as far as Palace Pier before Scott doubled back on himself, leaving Abby to continue her run to the marina and back. Without Scott slowing her down, Abby picked up the pace and pushed herself even further.

WITH A BLACK COFFEE in one hand and a slice of cold toast in the other, Scott talked to each team member in turn, catching up on the case.

Every member had this case as well as other smaller cases to deal with. Scott's need to do a review of each case meant many hours poring over each case file and the action points that each officer had undertaken.

Scott pulled a seat up alongside Helen. Her usual two-piece suit and blouse had been replaced by a pair of skinny jeans, white trainers, and a long-sleeved white top. With flame-red hair pulled tight in a ponytail, she looked young, trendy, and vibrant. Helen was proving to be a valuable officer who had transitioned seamlessly into the team after Sian's death.

She had arrived at a difficult time for Scott and the others. Shy and unsure of her position within the team at first, she had grown in confidence in the weeks following her arrival. Her key qualities had quickly come to light. She was tenacious, hard-working, methodical and, above all else, a team player. He had highlighted these key attributes to her in their PDP meeting, an opportunity for senior officers to look at the personal development plans of their team members. She had outlined both her five- and ten-year plan, which included going for her sergeant's exams, then pushing for inspector. In Scott's opinion, she would achieve her goals.

"Guv, I was looking into the backgrounds of the pastors," Helen said. "And I thought I'd have a look at the whole issue of asylum seekers coming onto our patch. Ironically, we've had no issues around asylum seekers in Brighton before."

Helen flicked through pages of scribbles. "I looked at some of the cases over the last few months, and uniform had quite a few run-ins with illegals who had been sleeping rough and begging on the streets, but nothing involving asylum seekers. Then Raj said something about how the dossers always end up in hospital as overdose cases or drunk. So I had a look at hospital admissions at the Royal Sussex."

Scott crossed his arms, unsure the direction that Helen was taking, but he admired her abstract thinking.

"Anyway, I spoke to the Royal Sussex. In the last twelve months, they've had seven adults admitted with pain in their abdomens. They've had more admissions than that, but I'm specifically referring to refugees claiming asylum or illegals. The interesting point here is that when they were X-rayed, they seemed to have foreign objects inside their bodies. And by that I mean things up their rectums or in the vaginal cavity."

Scott narrowed his eyes. "Smuggling? Drugs?"

Helen nodded. "Sounds like they're mules."

"What happened to them?"

"Of the seven, three had internal bleeding. All seven refused any further treatment and discharged themselves despite the pain. Hospital records noted that all individuals could hardly speak any English and looked terrified. Security staff tried to stop them leaving but couldn't. Police were called, but the individuals had already disappeared by the time officers arrived."

"Have you got any intel on what happened to them in the following weeks?"

"Five are unaccounted for. Two, a male and female, were found dead several days later after their visits. The female was found in Dymchurch in Kent, the male found near Folkestone."

Scott's mind raced as he considered the implications. *Why were they in Kent?*

"Post-mortem findings confirmed that both had severe injuries to their private regions."

"Good work, Helen."

Scott left her to look further into the cases. He left the station to follow one of his hunches.

Dolores Carter, with a visible passion and energy, had finished one of the weekly community sessions that she ran for the Afro-Caribbean community in Brighton. Scott waited by the doorway for Dolores to leave.

She exhibited a mixture of surprise and pleasure at seeing Scott.

"Hello, Inspector. I've been meaning to touch base with you. I've been pressurising the council and our local MP Alistair Woodman to grant me access to the families who have been taken to the detention centre."

"Any joy?" Scott asked.

Dolores shook her head and carried a box out. "Anyone would think I'm speaking a different language. Tried so many avenues and keep hitting a brick wall at every turn."

Scott offered a sympathetic nod. "You're not the only one. I've been getting the same brush-off. The Home Office swoop was a real blow to us. It's set back the investigation."

Dolores nodded sympathetically and smiled.

"I won't take up too much of your time, Dolores. I just wanted to ask, do you know of any refugees who have been paid to bring things into this country illegally?"

Dolores frowned as she loaded the box into the boot of

her car. "Um, I don't know, to be honest. It's not something I've heard of. You mean like drugs?"

"I'm not sure what I mean. To be honest, drugs seem to be the most likely option."

They discussed the viability of something like that happening.

Dolores went into some detail about the passage that many refugees take to arrive here, often by illegal or undetected means. The possibility of them bringing something into the country was an option.

"In my opinion, the majority of refugees are genuine and desperate for a better life, and being forced to be a mule of some sort would be unlikely for most. But let me make a few enquiries."

She promised that she would get back in touch once she had.

33

S cott returned to the office and rallied the troops around the incident board, keen to press on. A summary report from Matt Allan didn't lighten his load as Scott relayed the key points.

"We can now confirm the name of the second victim. As expected, it's Nathi Buhari, aged five. Swabs taken from his parents provided a DNA profile match. His parents have been informed, and they're devastated. We have a FLO with them at the moment. The left arm found on the beach near Palace Pier is Nathi's."

"I guess at least his parents have closure and can bury their child in peace after we've wrapped up this case," Abby said.

Scott agreed. As much as they needed that confirmation, the news itself took the wind out of the team's sails. Another young life tossed away like yesterday's rubbish.

Mike interrupted the silence. "Daniel Johnson's registration hasn't popped up on any ANPR cameras, guv. If he knows the area well, then it would be easy for him to stay off main traffic routes that have cameras. I've been examining the map. There are a couple of areas where I would go to ground if I needed to. But there is one area that I thought looked promising. It's a place north-east of Brighton. Towards Offham and not far from Lewes."

Mike moved over to the large map on the back wall.

"Most of the areas I looked at are close to roads or farmland. There's too much risk of being discovered by farmers." He pointed. "However, there are large swathes of dense woodland that run parallel to the B2116 between Offham and Plumpton. That place is as good a place as any to start looking. A stream runs straight through its centre. I reckon I could hide out for days there before being found."

Scott instructed Mike to take a couple of uniformed officers to carry out a provisional recce of the area in the hope of spotting Daniel's van.

The press appeal hadn't garnered any new information despite a flood of calls from concerned parents. A few callers identified strangers whom they hadn't seen before or neighbours whom they viewed with suspicion. No one had seen Xabi. For whatever reason, Xabi had disappeared into thin air. Scott was beginning to believe that Xabi had been spirited away by those who protected him. Each call, nevertheless, would be followed up for closure if nothing else.

The appeal itself might not have gathered much new information, but it had achieved their aim of it being heavily reported by the local and national papers and TV stations. BBC Sussex featured the appeal in some detail, even down to dispatching a reporter to the sites where both bodies were found, to bring live updates. Scott hoped that the press attention would keep the appeal in the public eye.

He continued the forensics update. "The organs and blood traces discovered in Daniel Johnson's room have been examined. The samples were sent away and processed overnight. We can now confirm that all the organs and blood belong to animals. A veterinary pathologist examined the evidence. She confirmed that the organs belonged to a cat, several species of birds, and the heart that Abby picked up belonged to a medium-to-large-sized dog."

Abby made a few notes. "Uniform are examining recent cases of animals being abducted, guv. I think we may have found their prime suspect."

Scott nodded his agreement. "A local resident out walking found some sort of den two days ago. We now believe it was being used by children. Because of its proximity to the Whitehawk estate and the location to where Michael's body was found, forensics were dispatched to examine the den in greater detail. They found sweet wrappers, biscuit wrappers, and half-empty bottles of fizzy drinks. Analysis of the evidence confirmed the presence of DNA that matched Michael and Nathi. Other DNA traces were found, but so far today we have had no hits."

"We know both boys knew each other and played together. Does that help our case in any way?" Raj asked.

Scott shoved his hands in his pockets and rattled some loose change. "Yes and no. Yes, it helps us to identify another place where the children hung out, but no, it doesn't bring us any closer to knowing who murdered them."

Raj banged his fist on the table. "Guv, this frustrates me. I'm sure there are people amongst the asylum community on the estate who know a lot more than they're letting on. But they're just too terrified to speak out."

Raj had a point, but trying to get through to them felt like a waste of resources.

Scott had already exchanged several heated phone calls with the Home Office. Any requests to get swabs from the six families who had been detained had been denied. The officials in charge also blocked any requests from Scott for release of the identity of the families being held at the two immigration removal centres close to Gatwick airport. He'd tried to circumnavigate the Home Office by contacting Brook House and Tinsley House immigration removal centres, but to no avail. Scott had been told that the release of information about who was housed at either centre required authorisation by the Home Office.

Scott tapped the pictures on the incident board. "Our focus must be on finding Xabi and Daniel Johnson. Daniel may have nothing to do with it, but I doubt it, and we have the CCTV stills that suggest he was the person who may have disposed of the arm near the pier. We're running out of time here, and we still have three children who are unaccounted for."

The fact that they hadn't found Pastor Xabi concerned him. Scott knew in his gut someone was harbouring the odious man. Pastor Mabunda seemed the most likely suspect, but several visits, plus one day where two uniformed officers were assigned to follow him, had revealed nothing. There was nothing in his daily routine that hinted at him being in contact with Xabi.

"The bodies of Michael and Nathi were found one mile apart, so Xabi could be in that area," Scott said. "But that's close to the Whitehawk estate, and supposedly, no one has seen him around there. If we go with Mike's suggestion, then the hunt for Daniel Johnson would take us in the opposite direction. So as a team we need to split up."

A consensus of nods showed that his team agreed with Scott.

"Mike, you stick with the area we agreed to check towards Offham. Raj and Helen, there's a large area of dense woodland beyond the den close to the Whitehawk. I want you to scan the area for any signs of Daniel or his van. Abby, I want you to call Barry Johnson. Press him on any favourite areas that Daniel might have mentioned before. Even if it seems trivial, or he only heard it in passing conversation, we need to know about it."

Scott's mobile rang as he wrapped up. It was Simon Young, the lecturer and expert on African culture.

Young's sharp demand that he visit him had Scott concerned.

34

Scott made his way to the university as a matter of urgency.

"What did he say?" Scott asked as he took a seat in Simon's office.

Simon's hands trembled as he tried to recall the conversation. "Erm, I...I...the man said, if you know what's good for you, stop snooping in our business. He muttered something in Zulu and said that if the police or I continued to look into tribal practices, we'd not see the end of the year."

Scott took down some notes. "Anything like this happened before?"

"Never."

"Did you recognise the voice?"

"I'm afraid not, Inspector."

Scott continued to quiz him. "Did they have an accent? English, African? Any other regional bias?"

Simon thought for a moment. "English. Perhaps London or the south-east. Well spoken."

"Could it be a crank call?"

"I guess it could be." Simon shrugged.

Scott asked more questions and reassured a visibly shaken Simon.

"I'm alarmed at the warning," Simon said. "I've been studying Africa and its people for over twenty years. Muti killings have absolutely fascinated me. Some people out there have such strong beliefs that these witch doctors and powerful spell makers can do absolutely anything. They are held in higher regard than traditional doctors, the police, stockbrokers, and bankers."

"Yes, I'm realising that." Scott checked his notes and assessed the evidence.

"They really are, Inspector. In traditional Southern African beliefs, it is assumed that there is only a certain amount of luck available in society. Each individual receives a portion of that luck. It is therefore believed that if another person is successful, then they have obtained an extra portion of luck via devious means, with the intervention of the supernatural. And a sangoma, a traditional witch doctor, fits the bill."

"I see."

"Any further update on your cases, Inspector?" Simon asked. Concern tinged his voice as he poured Scott a cup of tea. "Did you find who you're looking for? Was it muti after all?"

He was showing a little too much interest in his cases. Scott was unsure as to how much he should reveal. "We're still looking for those of interest to us and considering all possible motives. Can you think of areas where such killings could be carried out?"

"I don't think so, to be honest. From what I can gather, some muti killings back in Southern Africa have been done in front of the whole tribe. Others are being done in random locations after they have kidnapped someone. Just as many muti killings are conducted in quiet spots as in the open. The person often lights small fires or candles to mark out the ritual. In that type of setting, I guess they would need somewhere that's neither windy nor exposed."

"So indoors?" Scott asked.

Simon nodded and shrugged. "I guess. Somewhere where they are not going to be disturbed or attract attention. And I'm referring to this country, if that's the angle you're coming from with your questioning."

"That's helpful to know."

Simon reached for his laptop. "I was reading this article, and did you know muti is once again on the rise in South Africa, with more witch doctors wanting to serve people on the European continent? Demand is high. With a large African population living and working here, the doctors are targeting the UK. The Limpopo province alone once recorded two hundred and fifty muti murders in a single year."

He paused to flick through a document before continuing. "In 2013, a scandal broke when a hospital in Swaziland was accused of operating a black market in human body parts, to be used in black magic muti spells and rituals. Those in the know considered it an 'open secret'. They could literally buy from a shopping list. People came to the hospital from neighbouring regions to buy bones, hearts, brains, genital organs, tongues, ears, eyes, fingers, hands, feet, legs, arms, and any other part for muti medicines. If more of this is coming to the UK, then, Inspector, you have your work cut out."

"Two cases are enough for me," Scott replied, jotting down Simon's comments. He stood up to leave.

"Can I ask, were any of the children albino?"

Simon's question took Scott by surprise. "No, why do you ask?"

"Back in South Africa, albinos, known in Africa as 'ghosts'

or 'zeroes', are murdered for their particularly valuable body parts and skin. It's beyond comprehension. According to believers, an albino's arms, fingers, genitals, ears, and blood are prized for their especially powerful magic. For example, fishermen will weave albino hair into their nets to improve their catches whilst miners have splashed albino blood on the ground, worn albino muti charms or buried albino bones to 'attract' gems and gold to the surface, to improve their prospecting."

"That's a worrying aspect," Scott said. "I'll get my team to look into the number that called you. I'd also suggest being cautious for the time being. Please call us if you see anyone loitering around or acting suspiciously. And call me immediately if you get another call like today."

"I will do, Inspector. Thank you."

Scott thanked Simon for the tea and further information before leaving.

His mind overflowed with the insights he'd gained.

35

Daniel and Xabi drove out from Woodingdean in silence. Darkness surrounded them on all sides. An occasional car approaching from the opposite direction appeared like two cat's eyes in the distance. They'd scrunched their eyes when the beam from the headlights lit up the interior of the van. Each vehicle rushed by, leaving them in darkness once again.

Daniel had been given strict instructions to identify a spot that wouldn't be discovered for some time. Having scoured his maps, he'd settled for a location close to the Castle Hill national nature reserve, north of Woodingdean.

The heat inside the van had been turned up to a level that made it unbearable, but he dared not ask if he could turn it down. His mentor, Xabi, felt cold most of the time, but that was perhaps because he wore too little.

Daniel continued to drive along the unlit road that took them around long curving bends and an undulating landscape. Even with the headlights on, he could not get his bearings. The occasional lights from a farmhouse in the distance were all that shimmered out here.

His nerves tingled. His lips were dry with excitement, his hands sweaty, and his breathing short and sharp. The last few weeks of experimentation had taken him to a higher plane of understanding. His morbid fascination with death had been nurtured by the special one.

Daniel dared not look to his left. His mentor was a menacing figure, with penetrating eyes that could freeze him to the spot and drain him of his life force. Whenever Xabi pointed, his fingers twisted and contorted like the claws of a vulture. With his nails sharpened into talons, he had the ability to tear open a grown man's chest.

Xabi's grotesque appearance justified his reputation as a fearsome, mystical, powerful, and dangerous man. Men would fall at his feet and women would run, too scared to look him in the eyes.

Xabi hadn't uttered a word since they'd left the shed in the forest. Having completed the last act, his clients would be delighted with the outcome. Of that, Xabi was sure.

Daniel pulled into a lay-by. In the stillness of the night, they got out and travelled the last few yards on foot. The site was nestled in amongst a cluster of trees and large bushes, which offered the perfect camouflage. Daniel laid a small torch on the ground to illuminate the area, and drove the spade into the hardened earth. Months of a dry summer and little rain had left the ground parched and firm. The impact of it on the tip sent shock waves through his arms and into his shoulders. He cursed under his breath as he realised the difficult task that lay ahead.

After a few minutes, the beginnings of a shallow pit formed.

Sweat beaded from Daniel's forehead despite the chill of the night; moisture saturated his back as he toiled.

Several hours later he stood in the middle of the pit, its top edge in line with his thighs. His body ached, his shoulders were stiff, but he soldiered on under Xabi's watchful eyes. He had to make the chamber deep enough for the bodies.

He waited for his breath to calm before making his way back to the van.

Scrambling out from beneath the dense greenery, he paused. Daniel waited for his eyes to adjust to the darkness again. With little to see, he instead listened out for danger.

He made three trips in total. Each time he carried a small bundle wrapped in a blanket. One by one, he laid the bodies in the bottom of the pit. He returned to the van one more time and picked up a large plastic container that weighed little but carried precious cargo.

Standing by the edge of the pit, Daniel looked up at the sky and closed his eyes.

"*Amandla avela empilweni entsha*," he repeated for more than a minute.

He lifted the plastic container above his head before tearing the lid off and emptying the contents into the pit.

The thud of the heart hitting the bottom echoed loudly in the quiet. He shone his torch into the hole and illuminated the thousands of maggots that he'd also put there.

Xabi offered nothing more than a nod of approval.

Filling in the pit took less than an hour.

After, Daniel tore down some foliage from the bushes and laid them in a haphazard fashion over the turned earth. He straightened up, pleased with his night's work.

If the bodies were ever discovered, there would be little left after the maggots had finished their job. By that time, Xabi would be long gone.

36

The team arrived early to go over the final plans for the two sites they had identified yesterday. A ripple of laughter turned into raucous belly laughs when Mike, the last of the team, burst through the doors. Mike, never one to miss an opportunity to get down and dirty, had turned up dressed for an away day with the Royal Marines. He had on his black army boots, green combat trousers, and green sweatshirt. To finish his outfit, he wore a pair of green rubberised binoculars around his neck.

Mike must have raised a few eyebrows coming through the station.

Scott smiled. "Mike, you're looking for a nineteen-year-old man and evidence of him camping out. Not Osama Bin Laden."

The others fell about laughing.

"Guv, I don't know what type of terrain I will come across. And the last thing I want to do is stand out like a sore thumb. We were always taught to blend into the background." Mike looked down at his attire as if it made perfect sense.

Raj shook his head in bewilderment. "You blend into

something, but it won't be the background. You look more like a big, green pile of cow shit."

Mike pointed an accusatory finger at Raj. "Any time, mate...any time."

"Could you not get an army jacket to fit? One too many pork pies?" Raj continued.

"Enough, you two," Scott snapped. "This isn't a playground. Mike – or should I say Rambo – Helen, and Raj, you know what you're looking for. Get going now. Abby and I will situate between the two locations so that we can get to either site as fast as we can."

"THIS IS an absolute waste of time, since I'm sure the PolSA team covered some of this area," Raj mumbled as he trekked across the grassy incline.

Helen disagreed. "No, the search teams looked closer to the road and the estate. They didn't come this far. If we carry on in this direction, it will take us closer to the racecourse on our left and north beyond the Whitehawk."

"Yes, but we are heading to where the second lad was found. If Daniel Johnson is camping out somewhere and he's connected, then he'd be daft to go anywhere near that second crime scene. If you think about what the guv said, Johnson would be somewhere where he's not going to be spotted or disturbed. You have Warren Road, Bear Road, two crematoriums and a cemetery all within walking distance. He will not be here."

"You're probably right, but what happens if he is? Your arse would be in the firing line for not doing a proper search."

The weather was clear, mild, and dry. The hum of traffic

surrounded them; the familiar buzz of a light aircraft flying low attracted their attention for a few moments.

Other than a few joggers and dog walkers, Raj and Helen failed to spot anyone else. Nor did they find any evidence of anyone camping out, such as discarded rubbish, burnt-out campfires – nothing to suggest Daniel's presence. Despite spending the best part of two hours scanning the terrain, they continued their search.

THE LOCATION of Mike's destination took him north of Brighton into the Sussex countryside. Mike parked in Offham and headed west away from the village. He snaked his way through the forest, sticking close to a stream that cut through the centre. Despite his large frame, he made good walking progress. Something about being outdoors, following his instincts, and using his tracking and observation skills spurred him on.

He'd marked out a track just short of two and a half miles and followed a route that took him between Offham and Plumpton. Covering more than a mile, he hadn't seen a single living soul. He stopped every hundred yards, crouched down and checked his bearings on his map and compass, and scanned his environment through his binoculars before continuing.

The lush green vegetation provided the ideal background to blend in as he moved. The sound of the trickling stream that flowed just a few feet away masked the soft sound of his movements. The water was clean, fresh, and free-flowing. He occasionally saw the silhouette of fish swimming close to the streambed.

Something caught his eye that caused him to stop mid-step.

He crouched low and made his way towards the edge of the stream. Across some of the large rocks appeared to be entrails. Flies feasted, and Mike assumed they had been there for some time. But not far from the stones appeared to be bone fragments and the pelt of an animal.

Mike's heart quickened and pounded in his chest. He snapped his head up and scanned his surroundings.

Mike called Scott to update him before he continued.

He glanced over his shoulder, making out a rough trail that snaked off into the distance. Ground foliage and shrub matter had been pushed to the sides and trodden underfoot, as if used as a path to the stream on numerous occasions.

He placed each step carefully to avoid disturbing the ground or stepping on twigs that would crack and announce his presence. The makeshift path zigzagged through the trees before joining with another path that went deeper into the forest. Mike paused and looked through his binoculars for any sign of activity. With nothing obvious, he continued treading carefully. The path opened out into a clearing where about twenty yards ahead he saw a weathered brown shed.

He picked his way around the structure, looking for any openings or windows that would allow him to peer in. The door had a simple padlock that he prised off with relative ease using the butt of his torch. He smiled as he thought about how ineffective such locks were. He opened the door and stepped in.

Mike's smile was replaced with a grimace as a pungent foul smell assaulted his nostrils. He placed the crook of his elbow over his nose and glanced around the shed in horror.

A large A-frame had been constructed in the middle of the shed. What appeared to be the carcass of a dead animal was being hung by its back legs from bloodied ropes. Flies bounced off the four walls of the shed; several dozen more gorged on the fleshy remains. Mike batted the flies away, hoping that many would escape through the open door. To his right sat a stack of Tupperware boxes, each filled with items that raised Mike's curiosity.

Mike snapped on a pair of blue latex gloves and pulled the lid off the first container. He stared open-mouthed at the pair of eyeballs rolling around in a sticky layer of congealed blood. Other containers had similar macabre exhibits that took him by surprise. A hairy testicle sack, half a dozen chicken claws, and a furry foot – the latter Mike assumed belonged to either a rabbit or a cat.

A large container held a small animal skull that had been stripped back to the bone.

Needing out, Mike backed up into the fresh air, cleared his lungs and called Scott again.

THIRTY MINUTES PASSED before Scott and Abby arrived. With no road close by, they had parked some distance away and travelled on foot, guided by Mike's directions.

"What do we have?" Scott asked as he approached.

Mike shrugged. "I don't have a clue, guv. It looks like some chop shop for animals. Whoever's been here has been dissecting and storing animal parts."

Abby peeked in through the doorway. She scrunched up her nose and moved back. "Christ, it stinks in there."

Scott held his hand over his nose as he ventured inside. Mike's description couldn't have prepared him for the rancid, putrid, overpowering stench that clawed at him and sent waves of nausea shooting up his throat.

Scott counted twenty-three containers, and based on Mike's discovery, assumed that the rest carried similar items.

Back out in the open, Scott scouted the location. Forest

surrounded the shed on all sides, and it was well hidden from prying eyes.

"Abby, can you put in a call for forensics? We need to have the containers taken away and the shed given a once-over. We'll need a veterinary pathologist to confirm the origins of those samples."

"Will do, guv. I think we may have found the lair that uniform are looking for. I'll contact the constable who is handling the case."

"There's a locked box in one corner, guv. I don't know if you saw it?" Mike asked, nodding at the shed. "Do you want me to break it open? Or shall we leave it to forensics?"

"We might not have to break it, Mike."

Scott pulled a small plastic evidence bag out of his pocket. Inside was the set of keys he'd found whilst searching Daniel Johnson's room. They were worth a try.

Scott stepped into the shed again, followed by Mike. His eyes instantly watered from the overpowering smell. How anyone could sit in here was beyond Scott's comprehension.

The key fob had three keys of different shapes and sizes. The first key didn't fit. The second key did. Scott lifted the lid to find a roll of cloth, which he carefully placed on the floor.

Mike and Scott fell silent when Scott rolled out the cloth. An assortment of gleaming surgical utensils glistened in the semi-darkness of the shed. There were several scalpels of different shapes and sizes, fine metal picks, several pairs of scissors, metal tweezers, and several large knives, including one that Scott recognised as a machete.

"Looks like we've found the tools of the trade," Mike concluded. "Hopefully, they have Johnson's prints."

The two officers stepped back outside and ran through several scenarios.

"So do we do an obbo and wait for Johnson to come back?" Mike said.

Scott shook his head. "For a start, we don't know if it belongs to Johnson. The fact he was in possession of some keys relating to the box doesn't confirm ownership of the tools or shed. For all we know, he may have been just looking after the keys for someone else. At the moment, we can't prove that these keys belong to him. We also don't have the manpower to have officers sit here day after day, waiting for someone to return."

"Guv, we might not have to wait that long though."

"It's an unknown, Mike. Judging from the carcass in there, the shed was used in the last few days. But we have no indication how often it's being used, or when someone might return. The fact that there's a carcass hanging off an improvised A-frame in there makes me think that whoever did it left before completing the job. Perhaps they were disturbed or spooked and legged it before getting caught."

Abby joined them. "So what now?"

"I'm hoping that forensics finds DNA evidence in there that's a match for Daniel Johnson. In the meantime, whilst we are here, we'll spread out and see if we can find any other evidence." Scott lowered his voice. "For all we know, Daniel Johnson might be close by and watching us. Call it in, Abby, and let's see if there is a dog unit free. They might be able to pick up a scent."

37

The discoveries of the day before gave the team fresh hope. SOCOs had gone through the shed in meticulous detail. There was some debate last night as to whether the shed should be disturbed. Mike had argued it would have been better to leave it undisturbed in case the perp returned.

His suggestion, however, would have needed surveillance, which Scott knew wouldn't be approved. But Mike had assured him that a remote sensing camera fixed to a nearby tree would serve the purpose. Such cameras captured images triggered by movement, without the need for manpower. He explained that the technology was popular amongst hunters and wildlife managers.

Mike's military experience had also led him to use similar cameras in hostile territory where insurgents were positioned. Evidence of their movements could be captured on the ground, much in the same way that drones captured evidence from the air.

On the back of that, Scott asked Mike to speak to the techie team, to see if it could be organised as a matter of priority. Captured images of Daniel or Xabi could allow Scott to ask for extra resources.

Scott decided against leaving the shed intact. The containers had been examined, recorded, and removed to a location where a veterinary pathologist was examining them. Frustration dampened Scott's excitement when early indications suggested that there was no evidence of human remains.

Everything possible was being done to track down Xabi and Daniel. The press appeal hadn't yielded the expected results, and uniformed officers were on the lookout for both suspects. The lack of two suspects sitting in the cells troubled Scott. He added more findings to his notepad as he reflected on the case and chewed on cold toast.

He tapped the end of his pencil and glared at his scribbles. *Where are you, Xabi? Where are you hiding?*

"Guv, do you have a minute?"

Scott looked up from his food to see Raj in the door frame, smiling. Scott waved him in.

"I've been looking into the affairs of Alistair Woodman, and he has a chequered past to say the least."

The man's name was enough to pique Scott's interest. He straightened up as Raj sat down.

"I found several press articles that were buried in some other parliamentary stuff. It's on an anti-government blogger's website. It's called Free of Anarchy and run by a financial blogger called Freedom Joe." Raj lifted both brows. "Weird, I know."

He checked his notes before continuing. "Anyway, in the past, Woodman had been under scrutiny on suspicion of organising lucrative, backhanded trade deals with South African firms. I called his office and posed as a travel company conducting a survey. It turns out that he's been to South Africa over a dozen times in the past three years.

Whilst out there, he met frequently with tribal and business leaders."

Raj handed over a few sheets of paper. Scott glanced over each one. They were images pulled from Facebook and Google, with Woodman posing with tribal leaders and elders. There was nothing unusual in the images themselves, but Scott was drawn to the caption beneath the pictures. It stated that Woodman was meeting with Zulu tribal leaders.

Raj continued with his findings. "I believe it gives us grounds to investigate him further. You said yourself that there was something suspicious about him. Here he is rubbing shoulders with Zulu tribal leaders. And he's supporting the deportation of asylum seekers from South Africa, who are fearful of Zulu witch doctors."

Scott stared as he listened, trying to process the many loose strands that were currently creating confusion.

"He's a Member of Parliament, Raj. We can't just investigate him. Members have many privileges and rights that keep them well protected. To investigate Woodman's financial situation would require authorisation from a higher person. I doubt that the super would support me in that request, especially knowing Woodman's connection with CC Lennon."

"I know, guv. If you run with the accusations made on this blog, Woodman helps firms bring goods into this country without them paying excessive duties. He's supporting the undervaluing of goods. Now that's all circumstantial, but what if there's an element of truth? This blogger claims to have several key contacts within Parliament."

"Like informers?"

"Why not? We use informers. And there's an article here from a former junior member of staff within Parliament who blew the whistle on corrupt practices. They also highlighted the same revelations about Woodman. So that's two independent sources."

Scott tapped his pencil even harder as he crunched through the various scenarios. "So, Woodman helps firms profit. The question now is whether he takes a slice of those profits?"

Raj stood up and spread out all his findings over Scott's desk. "Guv, just look at all the information. My gut tells me that he's bent as a nine-bob note. But then I think that about most politicians. Self-interested, overinflated egos and money-grabbing bastards."

"That's a bit strong, Raj..." Scott smiled. "We're treading on thin ice when it comes to investigating politicians. Officially, we haven't a snowball's chance in hell of getting authorisation to investigate him or make further enquiries. And if we did, the response would be that Woodman is supporting and encouraging stronger trade links between the two countries. He'll have his reasons sewn up watertight."

Raj let out a huge sigh. "I know what you're saying, guv. But surely this smells bad to you? The whistle-blower spoke about rumours of bribes. And now the informer has been hushed up and is refusing to make any further comments. Apparently in parliamentary circles a fair number of accusations were made against Woodman in the past. Anything from inappropriate behaviour towards female colleagues, right through to taking backhanders from local and international businesses. Every accusation has been countered, rebuffed, and dismissed. Nothing seems to stick."

Scott shrugged. He'd walked the fine line of bending the rules on many occasions and had even crossed it a few times and lived to fight another day. But digging into the background of a politician? That was a whole new ball game.

They don't pay me enough to do this. This is career suicide, but...

Scott waved his hand in frustration. "Okay, okay. Find anything on Woodman. Discreetly."

Raj's grin stretched from ear to ear.

"Contact the Parliamentary Commissioner for standards to find out what information they are allowed to share publicly. Because as far as I'm aware, there is a registry of members' financial interests, and there's also a code of conduct for Members of Parliament. These may flag up what other interests and involvement Woodman has."

Raj nodded and jotted down his final note before dashing out of the room.

Scott sat back in his chair. The frame creaked beneath him as he pushed back and planted his feet on the table. He'd underestimated Woodman once. Never again.

38

Meadows tracked Scott down not long after his conversation with Raj. The DSI had a knack of popping up when Scott least hoped he would. If he wasn't paranoid about a tracker on his person before, he certainly was now.

His boss wanted reassurances that Scott wasn't going against the wishes of CC Lennon and investigating Alistair Woodman without concrete evidence. Scott was economical with the truth. He stated that Woodman was still on the radar, and that they were keeping an open mind into his financial dealings and points of contact.

Scott hoped it would pacify his boss and buy them some time. He knew he wasn't following procedure, but sometimes he couldn't help but to follow his gut. His mind was strong, but his heart was stronger. Perhaps that was why he kept getting into trouble.

Scott gathered the team around the incident board. It didn't paint a pretty picture. An assortment of pictures taken by SOCOs and the ones of the post-mortems highlighted the gruesome nature of the case they were dealing with. Pictures of Daniel Johnson, Pastor Xabi, and pictures of the shed just discovered now crammed the board. Various lines darted between them. The board looked a mess.

"Raj has uncovered some interesting stuff on Alistair Woodman," he told the team. "I'll leave it to him to update you after this briefing. In the meantime, we have three children unaccounted for. Their bodies haven't been discovered yet, so we should assume they are alive and being held somewhere. I spoke to Superintendent Meadows yesterday about the missing children, and the reason we haven't gone to the press about these three is because we have little to go on. We don't want to create widespread panic."

"We may never find them, guv," Abby speculated. The concerned look on the faces of the others suggested that they shared her view. "We can't be certain that they're still in the country. We're facing a wall of silence. We know six families are in detention, and the Home Office won't grant us access to them. For all we know, any one of the missing children could belong to the families who are being held."

Scott nodded in agreement. "It's a fair point. However, if any of those kids belong to those families, I expect the Home Office not to be that callous and that they would inform us. We need to keep pushing, chasing down all leads, and just keep digging." Staring at the incident board, he reflected on how those young victims would have been so scared for their lives.

The Home Office continued to deny open access. But Scott had persevered. His determination had finally paid off. Senior managers at the detention centres said they would consider the request if the Home Office relented. That was a positive step as far as Scott was concerned.

"Mike, how did you get on with the techie boys regarding the camera?"

Mike shook his head. "It's not the type of thing that they

keep. I've already made contact with a wildlife photographer, and he's going to let me borrow one. I'm picking it up this morning and heading straight over to set it up."

"Excellent. Good job, Mike. At some point today, I'm expecting to get initial forensics on the instruments that we found in the shed. That will help us to confirm who's used the shed. But I'm hoping that use of the camera will increase our chances of tracking down Daniel Johnson. Whoever used it has been there recently. A carton of milk in the shed had only been purchased in the last few days. There was a half-eaten sandwich, which, other than being stale, showed no signs of mould growth."

"Where were the items bought?" Helen asked.

"Sainsbury's. But trying to identify where they were bought is time-consuming, and time isn't on our side at the moment. Let's get out there and keep searching. Before we get on with it, any new evidence against *Pastor* Joshua Mabunda?"

An officer towards the back of the team confirmed that they'd been unable to find any recent links or contact with Xabi or the children since they went missing.

As SCOTT DROVE out of town alone, his earlier conversation with Meadows about Woodman raced through his mind. With no proof and no crime committed, Meadows had seen little value in investigating Woodman. Scott wasn't so convinced.

Members of Parliament had a knack of being very precise with their words and how they delivered them. Perhaps it was media training, or the fact that politicians rarely answered a question as expected. It was clear from his last visit with Woodman that Scott had touched a raw nerve. And like a bad itch, Scott wanted to keep scratching it.

The Oving was just as impressive as from his first visit as he was buzzed through the gates. In the brilliance of the afternoon sunshine, the house looked regal and elegant. It could have been the setting for a period drama. A horse and carriage parked outside, maids and servants scuttling about, and children playing on the lawn with a hoop and stick or skipping rope.

Stephen the butler answered the door, acknowledging Scott with a simple, small nod. He wore the same attire as last time and still looked tired and weary. He dropped his gaze.

Scott regarded him with concern and wariness. "Is Mr Woodman in?"

Stephen glanced at Scott before looking back, down the empty corridor. He did this several times, which Scott found strange. His inability to maintain eye contact troubled Scott.

"He's gone out, sir," Stephen said in the softest tone.

Scott stuffed his hands in his pockets. "Do you have any idea what time he might be back? I'd like to ask him a few questions."

Stephen shook his head once. "He said he was going to London on urgent business."

The man spoke so low, Scott struggled to hear him. He appeared timid on the inside as much as he did on the outside.

"Parliamentary business?"

"No, sir. He has a special bag that he takes to Parliament. That is still in his study. He took nothing with him today. He took a phone call just before he left. Said he needed to rush out immediately."

"And you don't know who that call was from?"

"No, sir." Stephen looked at the floor.

"Stephen, you seem a little worried. Is everything okay?"

The question appeared to take Stephen by surprise. He drew in a breath and held it; his shoulders stiffened. The man looked away, looked at Scott. He released his breath and nodded.

Given the visual cues, all was not well; Stephen had just lied. Something in the man's eyes conveyed a deeper pain, a silent call for help.

Scott pulled out his card and handed it to Stephen. "If you ever want to talk..."

Stephen took the card and went to close the door.

Scott returned to his car, the crunchy gravel beneath his feet breaking the silence and serenity of the space.

As he started the car, he saw Stephen peering through the half-closed door.

39

Heading home after the visit to Woodman's home, Scott sat in his favourite armchair and stared at his laptop screen. He had hoped to catch up on his Sky show recordings. The list multiplied by the day. With little free time, the list would grow even longer if he didn't pick them off one by one. With the TV volume set to low, it became background noise as his inquisitive mind preoccupied him.

He carried out a search on Alistair Woodman and stared at Google images of him. The man had a solid political background. According to one article, he had overturned a large Labour majority to win the seat of Brighton and Hove for the Conservatives. He had served in politics all his adult life, starting out as a young conservative. He didn't shy away from a challenge and often tackled local issues affecting his constituents. Woodman attended debates both locally and in Parliament and considered voting for new laws a privilege.

From Woodman's background profile, Scott learned he was a member of many committees, from government policy and new laws to wider topics such as trade and industry. The latter topic piqued Scott's curiosity. The man's understanding of regulations and authority and how trade and industry tariffs worked meant he would be well versed in how to bend the rules.

Digging a little deeper, Scott found articles and statements produced by Woodman. He advocated for fewer rules and regulations, which currently inhibited businesses from developing cross-border relationships.

Vociferous and unforgiving in his criticism of the trade and industry department, and in particular the minister in charge, he had accused them on many occasions of being the major hurdle to free trade. The Department for International Trade bore the brunt of his attacks. He called them antiquated – a bunch of dinosaurs who sat around the table, drinking tea, reading the *Times* newspaper, and sharing one brain cell amongst them.

The man has balls.

Scott stretched to relieve the tension in his shoulders. Cara had gone to bed early. When knee-deep in an investigation, he often struggled to switch off. His overactive mind, and that desire that every copper had of getting a result, regularly kept him up at night. He should have been upstairs curled up behind Cara's warm naked body instead of reading about Woodman.

He took another sip of Merlot; its warmth and richness soothed him. Despite his attempts to switch off enough so he could go to bed, his mind kept pulling up the horrendous images of Michael and Nathi. He couldn't begin to fathom why sacrificial killings were allowed and, according to Simon, were on the rise again.

He opened his inbox and scanned a few emails and articles from Simon. The content had an air of mysticism that pulled him in, absorbed into his mind, and raised his curiosity and fascination.

He read an article from 1994. It referred to the case of a fourteen-year-old boy who'd been murdered in Botswana and his body parts removed. The killing was widely believed to have been for muti, and the police even recovered some of the stolen organs as part of their investigation. However, before the organs were tested to identify them as human, the evidence was accidentally destroyed. It had led to accusations of police complicity in the muti murder. The case was never solved.

"Why am I not surprised?" Scott muttered.

One email from Simon caught his attention. It contained the subject line: "The case I mentioned to you the other day!"

In 2008, a rash of muti murders occurred in the Butterworth area of South Africa. It was believed that a local witch doctor had been responsible for a spate of murders in which body parts were harvested from the victims. The murders began with a nine-year-old boy, who was butchered in front of three friends by a man. Authorities later found the boy's body with his organs cut out.

Scott shook his head in disbelief.

The cases kept coming, one after another. Potential police corruption and falsified confessions had marred many of the investigations. The fact that people who carried out witchcraft were being touted as powerful people by the local immigrant community worried Scott. The risk of an explosion of muti killings coming to UK shores concerned him further.

40

The tyres screeched across the tarmac. And then time froze. Scott floated above the scene; Western Road spread out below him. He looked down. The BMW had come to a stop. From his vantage point, Scott saw the scene in minute detail.

Strands of Becky's mousey brown hair were splayed out on the road, a liquid turning it dark red.

The BMW had smashed into Tina and Becky, catapulting his wife over the bonnet. She had hit the windscreen and slid to one side before rolling on to the road. Becky had been dragged beneath the front of the car, just her upper half visible.

Scott watched as the driver reversed and drove around them. The car roared away down the street. His family lay in a heap. Broken. Dying...

"No!" Scott shouted. He sat up and groped around in the blackness.

Someone grabbed his wrists. He fought them. "Noooo!"

"Scott!" Cara, beside him in the bed, held on tighter. "It's just a dream, darling; it's ok, *shusssh*. Just a bad dream."

"Yes," Scott mumbled through gasps of breath.

Waking fully, he blew out a long breath and then lay down.

Cara wrapped her arms around him, and soon she was fast asleep again. Scott stared up at the darkened ceiling, unable to calm his pounding heart.

A dream, was that all it was? Or were the images more akin to a flashback? He'd never remembered that day so clearly before; his mind had done a sterling job of blocking out the worst parts of the memory. He blinked and tried to recall exactly what he'd seen.

A black BMW with a man behind the wheel. Dark hair. Caucasian? He couldn't be sure; the windows had been tinted. *Glasses...yes, he wore glasses!*

It would soon be four years since that day. He turned to the bedside table and the little picture frame on it. He smiled sadly at Becky's cheeky smile.

Ever since he'd lost them, Scott had been plagued with bad dreams and sweaty nightmares. In the beginning, he would spend half the night tossing and turning, often waking in a sweat, with the pillows on the floor and a tangle of duvet wrapped around his legs.

He still didn't buy the official report, which had recorded their deaths as a road traffic collision, or RTC, with the case being left open. But Scott had never considered what had happened to be an accident. It was more than that to him. Someone driving drunk or perhaps under the influence of drugs might explain why the driver had left the scene.

The hit-and-run driver had been travelling way too fast for Western Road. The driver hadn't hung around to see the full consequences of their actions. So far he had escaped punishment.

Scott had vowed to never let the case become a statistic.

I'll give it another look. He thought this as he succumbed to sleep once more.

THE AIR WAS thick with the scent of coffee as Scott came downstairs. Even though he wasn't hungry, the smell of toast that lingered in the air fired off a rumble in his stomach. Cara had woken before him and had prepared breakfast for both of them.

He walked up behind her as she was finishing the eggs, and looped his arms around her waist. A thin T-shirt she wore separated him from her naked body.

"Morning, beautiful," he said, planting a soft kiss on her neck. "This is a nice surprise. I could get used to this."

"Just doing my bit, Scottie. You must have had a late one last night. I don't remember you coming to bed."

"Yes, sorry. I had some research to do, and before I knew it, it was gone one a.m."

"Did it help?"

Scott let slip a laugh. "Yes, it was about a woman who wanted to become pregnant. She went to a sangoma, which is what they call a witch doctor. The man provided her with a magical belt to wear. Dangling from the belt were children's fingers and penises. She was made to drink a concoction she believed contained human blood and fat, and she was given a piece of flesh that she believed had come from a human organ, perhaps a heart. She sliced small pieces from the flesh each night and fried them."

Cara stopped cooking the eggs and turned to Scott. "Seriously?"

"Yeah, I'll show you the article."

Cara playfully punched him in the arm. "I mean, seriously, do we have to talk about this before we've even had breakfast? Do you ever switch off?"

Scott smiled and apologised. He grabbed the orange juice from the fridge.

Cara looked at Scott, with a look of concern. "Hey, are you okay after...last night?"

He gave her a kiss on the cheek and brushed off the incident. "I'm fine, babes. Thank you. I've not had many nightmares recently, so it spooked me."

Cara smiled sympathetically and blew him a kiss, then returned to finishing the food.

Scott wasn't due in until mid-morning. Having breakfast with Cara had given him a different appetite as he admired her curves beneath the tight-fitting T-shirt. Her pert nipples poked through and stirred his desire for her.

Unable to resist any further, he led Cara back to bed, where they made love, and then showered together.

41

Scott's mood improved as the morning continued. Mike had called to say that they'd had more feedback on Daniel Johnson. The camera that Mike positioned yesterday had been triggered late last night. Mike had gone there to retrieve the camera that morning and found images that resembled a person who looked like Daniel Johnson going into the shed. Forensics had also confirmed that the instruments discovered had Daniel's DNA on them, along with another set of unknown prints.

Both pieces of evidence were just what they needed. It placed Daniel Johnson in the shed as well as having used the instruments to mutilate animals. A further startling piece of evidence raised the stakes further. Human hair fibres had been discovered on one wall, stuck to blood smears. Comparisons made against DNA samples from Michael, Nathi, and the national database had so far proven unsuccessful.

Scott strode into the office with a strong bounce to his step, giving the team the only indication of the morning he'd had. In reality, he preferred to keep his private life just that,

private. With the case turning a corner and, more importantly, his personal life in a good place, his headspace was
clearer. Much of that was down to Cara. Truth was, he
couldn't wait to see her again. He couldn't imagine life
without her; he would spend every minute by her side if
given the choice.

Abby's excited voice grabbed Scott's attention. Her enthusiasm buoyed him.

"Guv, good old Dolores Carter has come up trumps for us.
She's been working really hard on our behalf to prise any
information from the remaining asylum seekers. She's got
through and gained the confidence of one particular individual. They weren't willing to come in with her, so we'll just
have to take her word for it until we can persuade them to
come in and make a statement."

Scott grabbed a seat beside her. "Credible though?"

"I think so. Anyway, Xabi had been arranging for asylum
seekers to come into this country. He would smooth the way
for them to enter the country. In return, he forced them to
bring gold smuggled on their persons. They would either
have to stick it up their rectum or vaginal cavity, and it would
be retrieved once they arrived here."

"That would explain the cases at the hospital."

"Makes sense, guv. I doubt they wanted to be searched.
They disappeared before being examined. And we know
what happened to a few of them."

"And Dolores has no idea where the pastor is?"

"Not as far as we know, guv. I agree with you, Xabi is being
shielded by someone. Of course, this witness Dolores found
could be too frightened to tell. He's putting his life on the line
by revealing this information. Dolores said he just kept going
on about how they're all promised a new life in the UK if they
smuggled gold in."

"Scott!"

Meadows's booming voice thundered across the open office as he entered through the double doors. Everyone turned to watch him approach. His stern expression and furrowed brow suggested that this wasn't a friendly visit.

"Get yourself down to the Whitehawk. Two houses that held asylum seekers have just been firebombed. Firefighters are still sifting through the debris for bodies. Let's hope they find none."

The team exchanged glances and looks of confusion.

"I saw this coming, Scott," Meadows added. "Your going in heavy-handed hasn't helped. I warned you that racial tensions were high, and that we had to go in softly."

"No disrespect, sir, but I hardly think we went in heavy-handed. I think we have been very considerate to the needs of the community. We've been dealing with a double murder, sir. Could the firebomb attack be down to something else?"

"Oh, it's racially motivated. Red swastikas were daubed on the outside walls. There's concern for the other asylum seekers. We have Syrians, Afghans, Eritreans, Sudanese, Iranians, Pakistanis, the Nigerians, and the Iraqis. They'll all be worried now. I've just been speaking to the Brighton and Hove refugee and migrant forum. They estimate that we have between three hundred and four hundred asylum seekers in the Brighton and Hove area. We can't protect them all, and we certainly don't want more body bags."

"It's the actions of the Home Office and Woodman that are stirring up racial tensions – sir."

Meadows glared at Scott. The tension between them prickled the air. "Keep the Home Office and Woodman out of the equation. I've already told you that the chief constable wants Woodman left alone. You bring the evidence that Woodman is anything other than clean, and I'll back you to the hilt. Until then, sort out this mess on the Whitehawk."

With that, Meadows departed, leaving bewilderment in his wake.

"SOMEONE LEFT THE GAS COOKER ON," Abby quipped as they stared at the burnt-out remains of two terraced houses.

The roofs had crumbled and made visible thick beams of wood now blackened and charred from where the flames had licked at them. The ruins still belched smoke, and Scott could see the faintest glow of embers as the firefighters continued to douse the last pockets of flames. Black choking dust hung in the air and invaded his lungs as he stood on the pavement. Nothing had escaped the fire, merciless in its destruction. Glass littered the ground where the windows had broken and lay blackened.

"Not much left. The council will be pissed off," Scott remarked as he looked around at the gathering crowds.

Mike joined them after having spoken to the officers first on the scene. "Firefighters reckon it was arson. There's a smell of accelerant from behind the doors. Chances are petrol was poured through the letter boxes and lit. There are rags on the floor just inside each doorway. The firefighters have completed their search. There are no occupants."

At least Scott could be thankful for that. The fire had been no accident. The charred shells were much more than a couple of burnt-down houses. The invisible messages on the blackened walls carried warnings.

"The locals don't seem too concerned," Abby remarked, glancing at a crowd being kept at a distance by PCSOs. Residents gathered in numbers, watching with morbid fascination. Some laughed, sharing a common joke, whilst others gossiped in hushed tones.

"Yes, I noticed that," Scott said, sighing. "Question is who did this? I can't imagine getting any useful information from that lot. It could be kids, a disgruntled resident, or someone else." He looked at the tangled mess of what had once been homes for those seeking sanctuary. "The press are going to have a field day," he mumbled.

Scott turned to see his favourite reporter, Tracey Collins from the *Argus*, pushing through the crowds.

Door-to-door enquiries in the vicinity of the arson attacks had offered few clues. The majority of those questioned hadn't seen or heard anything. One or two residents were more vocal, expressing that the immigrants shouldn't have been let into the country in the first place, let alone given priority over housing allocation.

It was what Scott had expected. He sensed the brittle atmosphere could snap at any moment. Fire investigation officers from the fire service were conducting a detailed search of both properties to identify any further evidence.

Scott had avoided Tracey Collins's pleas for an interview or exclusive. Miss Collins had a charming disposition and always dressed professionally. With her blonde hair tied back in a ponytail, her smooth complexion offered the perfect backdrop to a brilliant, pearly-white smile. She was petite, slim, and attractive in Scott's opinion. He had rebuffed her suggestion on more than one occasion for a drink after work to form – as she put it – a stronger working relationship. He was too long in the tooth to fall for that ploy. Mike or Raj, on the other hand, wouldn't need to be asked twice.

Helen and Raj had been working back in the office whilst the rest of the team attended the fire. Scott returned to the office to see Helen had left a note on his desk.

He read the note twice in case his eyes were playing tricks on him.

Two of the firms that Alistair Woodman had been helping were gold importers.

Scott fired an email back to Helen, asking her to dig up anything on those two firms. Excitement rippled through Scott. He was certain that there was a connection between the MP and his vested interest in the asylum seekers.

42

Scott went to see Meadows immediately, keen to share the information on Woodman's business dealings.

"What makes you so sure?" Meadows asked.

"Sir, we have at least two asylum seekers dead, their private parts crudely cut out. Two of the seven had attended hospital with crippling pains. We also have an asylum seeker who's come forward to say that Pastor Xabi used them as mules to smuggle gold into the UK. Add to that, we have Woodman's support for deporting asylum seekers, some of whom have been used as mules. And Woodman is helping gold importers."

"That's all well and good, Scott, but we have nothing on paper." Meadows tapped each reason out on separate fingers. "You have no formal witness statement. You have no paper trail linking Woodman to Xabi or to the gold importers. It's too tenuous at the moment. Get me that information, and I'll escalate this for you."

Scott was about to continue when Meadows's phone rang. He answered and listened before hanging up. "You're needed downstairs. Uniform has made a sighting. They believe it to be Daniel Johnson."

SCOTT TOOK the stairs two at a time. His heart pounded in his chest; his thoughts tumbled through his mind. The case was careering in all directions. He burst through the doors of the incident room to see the team gathered around Abby's desk.

"Guv, a patrol car reported in to say they've had a sighting of a man matching Daniel Johnson's description," she said. "They are following at a discreet distance and waiting for further instructions from us. The suspect is carrying what appears to be a large blue IKEA bag over his shoulder. Shall I tell them to move in?"

The team was poised for Scott's next command.

"Tell them not to move in. Just to follow him until we get there. They can't lose him. Make that bloody clear to them."

The team raced to their desks and grabbed radios and anti-stab vests. They were out of the building in less than five minutes. A sense of urgency spurred everyone on as they raced down the stairwell and into the station car park at the rear.

Two blue job cars screamed through town, the wail of their sirens bouncing off the tall buildings. The blue flashing grille lights signalled their intention as cars and buses scrambled to clear a route. Scott and Abby led in the first car, followed by Mike, Raj, and Helen in the second.

The running commentary given by the uniformed officers confirmed that the suspect was now travelling by van and heading north out of town. A PNC check confirmed the owner was Daniel Johnson. The news heightened the tension in both cars as they closed in on one of their suspects. Once out of the city centre, the convoy raced along the A27. The patrol car confirmed that they were heading in the direction of Offham and were minutes away.

Scott and the team were a good fifteen to twenty minutes behind. Abby put in a request for a NPAS unit overhead. Haywards Heath was the nearest, but they were tied up on a job. Not encouraged by the news, Scott pressed his team on.

The patrol car came to a stop outside of Offham. The suspect, though not positively confirmed as Daniel, had pulled up several hundred yards ahead and had made off on foot into the edge of the forest, still carrying the large bag. Scott instructed the officers to follow on foot, but at all costs to avoid being seen. Scott hoped that the suspect would head towards the location of the shed once again, where they could contain him. With little daylight left, the team needed to act fast or risk losing Daniel in the darkness.

Scott and the second car pulled up behind the patrol car. He and his team grabbed some torches before heading off on foot, whilst maintaining radio contact with the officers following the suspect. The team zigzagged one way and then went another way, through trees and out into open land before heading back into the dense, darkened woodland again.

The team found the two uniformed officers looking around. "We've lost him, guv. He went all over the shop. One minute he was here; next minute he was there. And then he went around some tall trees and bushes, and by the time we followed up behind, there was no sign of him." The officers held out their hands apologetically. "It's just like he disappeared." Dejection and embarrassment showed on their faces.

"We know where he is going," Scott said. "You head back to the road and keep an eye on his van."

Scott's team spread out in a thin line and continued to pick their way through the forest. Mike guided them, following the path he had trodden on his last visit. It twisted and turned through corridors of trees that disappeared into the gloom until Mike reached a bend. The overhead canopy created a heavy gloom that made it hard for the officers to see. Mike darted to his right; the others followed quickly. The track opened out into a clearing. Up ahead was the shed.

Scott reached the shed door and opened it.

"Fuck!"

The suspect had already been and gone. Mike and Raj scanned the surrounding area in case he was hiding out. Abby and Helen ventured into the shed. The suspect must have been spooked by the absence of the hanging animal carcass and the various Tupperware containers that had all been removed. Various paraphernalia had been scattered, as Daniel had clearly left with a sense of urgency.

Abby ran out of the shed and headed to the forest edge. Loud retching sounds came from behind a bush.

Helen followed out after her. She explained to Scott, "She found the head of an animal in the corner."

Scott scanned the shed floor and saw tea lights, wine glasses, red velvet cloth, a box of matches, and what appeared to be an animal skull with small antlers.

"At least we know the contents of his IKEA bag, and it wasn't some matching IKEA cushions. All the things you would need for a sacrificial ritual."

Scott was just about to radio the uniformed officers when his radio crackled to life. The suspect had returned to his van with the blue bag folded under his arm and was now on the move and being followed by the patrol car. Scott instructed Mike to stay put by the shed until extra officers arrived in case anyone returned.

The team was back on the blues as they raced back towards Brighton. Scott listened to the running commentary given by officers. Scott was frustrated that the suspect appeared to be one step ahead of them. Rush hour traffic had begun to build up in town, slowing their progress. The town centre had a reputation for being congested most of the time, and it was certainly living up to it as the car crawled. Scott and the team made their way to Preston Park, where the suspect had left his vehicle and was now sitting on a bench, looking around nervously and glancing at his phone.

Tension ratcheted up as Scott and Raj split to take their cars in different directions, to circle around Preston Park. They maintained covert obs on the suspect. With darkness creeping in, maintaining a clear line of sight from the vehicles would prove difficult. Scott held his position out of sight whilst the other car continued to drive back and forth.

Helen came on the radio to say that the suspect was back in his vehicle and on the move, heading north. She had exited the car and walked past the suspect as he sat on a bench. She ID'd him as Daniel Johnson. They followed.

According to Raj, Daniel was weaving in and out of traffic, overtaking stationary traffic and jumping through red lights. The threat to life worried Scott as Raj struggled to keep up with Daniel. Scott was positioned on the wrong side of Preston Park and was attempting to catch up. Daniel's erratic driving was causing pedestrians to jump out of the way, and oncoming cars to swerve out of his path.

The radio sprang in to life. It was Raj, and Scott heard the words he dreaded most. "I've lost him, guv. I repeat, I've lost him. I'm circling around to see if he dipped down a side road."

Scott caught up with Raj and agreed on the areas they would drive around. For all they knew, Daniel could be holed up in a side street waiting, or he could be halfway out of town by now.

Twenty minutes had passed when the search came to an abrupt halt. Confusion erupted over the airwaves once again.

Mike whispered, "He's here... He's here!"

Abby gave Scott a startled look.

"Who's there, Mike?" Scott asked. An uncomfortable pause followed. "Come on, Mike, talk to me."

It seemed an eternity before Mike responded, in another soft whisper. "It's an IC3 male at the shed. I'm too far away to see who it is. He's carrying a suitcase. Stand by."

Scott stared at his handset as if it would talk on its own.

"He's stopped outside the shed... He's peering in. Wait..." There was another pause that seemed to go on for minutes. "He's looking around. I'm keeping my head low. He's...he's going in."

Abby mouthed the words Mabunda or Xabi to Scott.

Scott shrugged, not knowing the answer. "Have uniformed backup arrived?"

"Confirmed. We have another officer positioned in the treeline on the other side of the shed."

Scott thumped the steering wheel in anger. "We're on our way. They are giving us the runaround."

It was time to call in the cavalry. With such a large geographical area to cover, the odds were stacked against them. Scott instructed the control room to send more units to back them up and head towards Offham.

"Guv, the IC3 is leaving," Mike said. "I repeat, the IC3 is leaving. Await further instructions. Over."

"Any further update on the ID?"

"That's a negative, guv. It's way too dark."

Scott glanced at Abby.

"We won't get a second chance, guv," she said.

As if reading Abby's thoughts, Mike came over the airwaves again. "This is stupid. We're moving in, guv. We can't afford to let him get away."

"Mike, I'm not comfortable with that. You don't know if

he's armed." A flashback of what had happened to Sian raced through his mind.

"It's a risk I'm prepared to take, guv. The other officer is circling around to my position now. We've worked too hard. If this is Xabi... We have the whole of Brighton nick looking for him, and he's right in front of me."

"Okay, Mike. Approach with caution. If you're able to apprehend him easily, then do so. If he resists or is carrying, you back off immediately, do you understand? We are on our way. I repeat, we are on our way."

MIKE CREPT out from behind some bushes and approached with stealth. He remained low, taking one footstep at a time, careful to avoid detection. It reminded him of his days in Afghanistan when a suicide bomber had crept up close to where a British Army unit was helping monitor a roadside checkpoint. The suicide bomber had a child with him, and a sniper's shot would have been too risky.

Mike had abandoned his rifle and crept out of the building and down the road. He had worked his way through the broken ruins until he came within feet of the bomber. Each foot had to be carefully placed to avoid disrupting the rubble and broken glass, which would have revealed his presence. With his knife in one hand, he'd inched closer. He'd gotten the man's head in a tight headlock and drawn his blade across his neck. He'd heard the man take his last breath.

That day he had saved a young Afghan boy's life and a patrol of eight British Army personnel and their Afghan counterparts.

Back in the present, he put his army skills to use. Mike crept up on the man and shoulder-charged him, sending the suspect flying to the ground. He attempted to throw himself on top of the man before he could get up, but the suspect rolled over on to his back and blew some dust through a small six-inch pipe into Mike's face.

In that fleeting second, Mike saw the contorted, disfigured face of Xabi glaring up at him.

The dust took hold, and Mike fell onto his back. He rolled around and screamed in pain. His eyes stung as if he had been pepper sprayed. His lips tingled; the inside lining of his nose burnt; he coughed and spluttered as the substance scratched and irritated his throat.

He tried to open his eyes, but the searing pain stopped him. Unsure of Xabi's location, his mind swirled. Mike heard Xabi mutter something in a foreign language as he slipped in and out of consciousness. Every one of his senses urged him to get up and fight, but his face felt like he had been stung a thousand times.

The officer ran forward. "Police, stay where you are!"

The beam from his torch swept from left to right in an attempt to spot the assailant. The officer raced off after him into the trees.

As Mike writhed on the ground, Xabi disappeared into the darkness of the night.

43

Feeling pleased with himself, Daniel traipsed back through the woods and made his way towards the shed. The plans for a meetup hadn't gone the way he had hoped. With the police having discovered his shed, he knew they would be closing in on him. They'd made it so obvious when the woman had walked past him on the bench. The daft bitch had reached for her radio, thinking he couldn't see her action.

Heading back to the shed, Daniel decided to clear anything of value there before moving to a new location. The quicker he did that, the quicker he could be away, just in case they were still following him.

Within sight of the shed, a sound stopped him mid-step. A moaning, wincing sound that at first, he couldn't make out. Perhaps it was an injured animal. Maybe he'd have one last chance to practise his new craft. He still had a large penknife in his pocket. It wasn't perfect for the job. It would make it messy, but it would be fun.

The sounds grew louder as he crept through the undergrowth. He approached with caution. If it was an injured animal, he didn't want to frighten it off.

He peered into the abyss. The darkness of the woods was chilling, haunting, and shadowy. As his eyes strained to focus in the blackness, he saw the source of the noise. It was longer than he thought, perhaps a deer. They were about that size. And then he saw with clarity. Human legs.

Daniel stood above the large man, who groaned in his semi-conscious state. As the man gripped his face in his hands, a muffled moan erupted from between his fingers.

Daniel couldn't believe his luck. He had experience of killing animals and children, but had never tried with a grown man. His heart quickened, and his mind raced with the endless possibilities to learn.

Damn, damn. Time was against him. He wouldn't be able to prepare in the way he had been taught. He would have to improvise. Yes. Improvise.

He raced to the shed and looked for anything he could use. Grabbing what he needed, he made his way back. The man had pulled himself into a foetal position, tucking his knees tight to his chest.

Using all his strength, Daniel grabbed the large man by his ankles and dragged him inch by inch towards the nearest trees. The man's heavy weight and bulk proved a challenge. Daniel puffed out large breaths of air. Each step back took him closer to the cover of a large tree. The man was incapacitated by whatever noxious substance he'd come into contact with. The hulking man was at his mercy.

Daniel heaved the man up into a seated position and leant him back against the tree. With the rope from the shed, he secured the man's hands behind him and around the tree trunk and tied his ankles together.

The man groaned once again as his head lolled forward. Daniel carefully lit several candles and positioned them in a circle around the base of the tree. He placed the animal skull with small antlers to the left of his victim, a small bundle of herbs placed to the right. Daniel reached into his back pocket and pulled out his penknife. Its silver blade flickered in the candlelight.

"*Amandla avela empilweni entsha*," he repeated as he looked up at the darkened sky. His chants became louder as he summoned the gods.

Oblivious to his surroundings, and in a trance of his own, Daniel missed the transmission coming through the man's radio.

———

SCOTT AND ABBY pulled up by the forest edge. Approaching blue lights signalled the backup that Scott needed was here. To his relief, he could hear NPAS in the distance. Raj and Helen were sixty seconds away, having tagged on behind a squad car as it carved its way through the traffic.

"Mike, are you okay? I need a sit rep from you now." Only crackling static fired back at Scott. The signs weren't good. "Mike, come in. If you can't talk, press the red button."

Still nothing.

The officer in pursuit of Mike's assailant finally came back over the radio. "Suspect lost."

Scott swore.

The eerie darkness of the night sky heightened Scott's tension. The fear he felt was clawing at him, waiting to take over. He let out a slow, controlled breath, and attempted to loosen his body as he and Abby made their way over the uneven ground.

His eyes moved with alertness and stress; his hands remained clenched out of fear for Mike. Mike's lack of response worried him. *Not again.*

A vision of Sian, one of his officers, whom he'd lost after she was stabbed by a suspect, sent waves of dread over him. In his frozen state of mind, one thought remained: *Please be alive.*

With the support of several other officers and a dog handler, a new sense of urgency pushed him from a walk to a run. Abby picked up the pace and charged ahead. Scott puffed and panted to keep up with her. Darkness and unfamiliarity hampered their trail into the forest. Scott stumbled; his arms wheeled for balance. Rustling in the bushes surrounded them as startled nocturnal animals raced for safety. Beams of light from torches criss-crossed the way ahead.

Hope came at last as a broad finger of light beamed down to the ground from the powerful searchlight of an NPAS 15 helicopter that was guiding them to the location. The chopping sound of the blades disturbed the air as it whirred overhead.

Scott could hear the heavy panting of the K9 as it strained on the long lead. They weaved through the trees. The blackness and density of the woods brought on a bout of claustrophobia. The knotted roots crossing over the narrow path they followed made it uneven and treacherous. Low-hanging branches forced them to duck at intervals.

Up ahead, the first signs of light gave them hope. Daniel's chanting was drowned out by the whirring helicopter blades, the K9 barking, and officers shouting.

Startled, Daniel rose to his feet and ran off into the darkness. His departure came to an abrupt end when the handlers released the K9. The dog made light work of covering the thirty to forty yards between it and the suspect. A yelp and scream, followed by, "Get it off me! Help!" confirmed Daniel's capture.

Within minutes officers flooded the clearing as more sirens wailed in the distance.

"Mike, talk to me, mate. Mike!" Scott shook Mike's shoulder to rouse him. Abby checked him over.

"Ambulance is on the way, guv," Abby screamed over the noise. "There are no open wounds or blood loss. But his face is swollen. Drugged?"

His colleague and friend could only manage an anguished groan as whatever substance he had been given still incapacitated him.

"Looks like it. There are no facial or head wounds. And he's drifting in and out. He's alive, and that's the main thing."

"Mike isn't exactly a small chap, so how was he over-powered?"

"We'll find out once he's been taken to the hospital."

44

"Guv, this is Dr Murray, a psychiatrist from the Royal Sussex County Hospital. He checked Daniel Johnson over."

Scott shook Dr Murray's hand and leaned against the wall outside the interview room. "So, is he fit for interview?"

Dr Murray referred to his notes. "In my opinion, yes. Willing to talk, lucid, requested a solicitor. You may find it hard to gain his full cooperation. He's preoccupied with secrecy and order. He's a fantasist, wrapped up in his own world, but where his thoughts are logical as far as he is concerned."

DANIEL JOHNSON WAS AN ODD-LOOKING CHARACTER. He had a bowl haircut; his brown hair was untidy and greasy. As Scott stared at him, he noticed how Daniel's small eyes made him look cross-eyed. He had a wide face, which sharpened to a pointy jaw. His mouth was twisted into what looked like a permanent scowl.

Abby did the introductions and cautions for the tape. Daniel sat alongside the duty solicitor. It was the same rotund, po-faced man who had been present in other cases.

"Daniel, were you responsible for the body parts that were discovered in your room and in the shed?" Scott asked.

Daniel's eyes flickered between Scott and Abby.

"Yeah. I captured, killed, and dissected them. More than twenty animals, ranging from birds to household pets."

It appeared that Abby had found Samantha Huxtable's animal abductor.

"Why did you do it?" Scott asked.

Daniel shrugged, saying, "Anatomy has always fascinated me. Different size animals have different sized organs. The little sparrow's heart is no bigger than the size of a garden pea. The heart of a dog is just a little bigger than a tennis ball. It's their texture, the warmth." His eyes widened. "Man, it's weird."

Daniel went into detail about the gruesome processes he carried out on the different animals that he caught. For some, he would cut off their heads and cut out their brains. Others he would slice down the abdomen, remove the vital organs and dissect them. According to him, he enjoyed skinning animals the most. He went on to outline the intricate processes needed to separate the skin from the underlying flesh, bone, and muscle in one piece.

Abby made notes.

Daniel continued to talk in a matter-of-fact way as if he were chatting to someone down at the pub. He showed no remorse but an extreme fascination.

Scott pushed a CCTV still image across the table and tapped the photograph. "We believe the person in this picture is you, standing by the edge of Palace Pier."

Daniel stared hard at the picture; a smile broke on his face. "It looks a bit like me, but I don't think it is."

"You see, we think it is. The images that we have show someone matching your description walking onto the pier with a carrier bag that appears to be bulky. Ten minutes later we catch that same person leaving with no bag. We believe that you were responsible for dumping the arm of five-year-old Nathi Buhari in the water." Scott put a series of new stills on the table.

Daniel's eyes widened as he glared at two pictures of Nathi. The first depicted a young boy smiling, the second the crime scene, where his body was found.

"Not much of him left, is there?" Daniel tilted his head, seeming to show a morbid curiosity with the crime scene.

Out of the corner of his eye, Scott looked at Abby. She rolled her eyes as if to suggest "what a weirdo".

Scott changed tack. "Can you tell us about Pastor Mabunda?"

Daniel shrugged. "He's all right. He ran a club for the asylum seekers at the hall that me and my dad manage."

"That *you* manage? I thought it was just your dad?"

He shook his head. "No, I helped my dad out quite a lot when I was around. Whenever I went camping, he did a fair bit of it on his own."

"Did Pastor Mabunda ever do anything to make you believe that the children who attended the community centre could come to any harm?"

"Nah, he's too soft. He's too jumpy and nervous."

Scott pushed further. "So, have you always been into stuff like witchcraft and voodoo?"

"Sort of. I've always wondered what all the voodoo and occult stuff was about. I read a lot of stuff like satanism, paganism."

"What do you know about sacrificial killings or ritual killings of humans?"

Daniel's eyes widened. Scott had hit on something that spiked the suspect's interest.

"Ritual killings carry a lot of weight, a lot of power," Daniel said. "You can cast spells, both good and bad, by sacrificing a human to the gods."

"And how did you come to hear about that?" Abby interjected.

Daniel wasn't focusing on either officer. His eyes were glazed over, as if he were in a trance. "The internet, books, lots of different places."

"Did anyone else teach you this?" Scott asked.

A smug grin broke out on Daniel's face. He focused on Scott. "He said you would be looking for him. But no one has caught him yet. He's far too powerful. You blink and he's gone." He snapped his fingers.

"Who are you talking about, Daniel?"

"You know exactly who I'm talking about. The other pastor. Pastor Xabi." Daniel pointed a finger at Scott. "The most dangerous man you'll ever meet."

The suspect then explained how he had been introduced to Xabi when Pastor Mabunda ran the community centre group. He recalled the first occasion when Xabi turned up, and the terrified looks on the faces of the asylum seekers. Many had only been in the country a few hours.

"They were shitting themselves. I don't know if it was because of the way he looks. He looks like a monster that's been sheep-dipped in a vat of acid." Daniel laughed.

"And what happened next?" said Scott.

"Well, some of the newbies were summoned by him to a room, and then they left. They were driven off in a black van, and I never saw them again at the community centre."

"And you have no idea why he was taking them away?"

"Not in the beginning. He saw me reading a book about the occult and all this voodoo stuff. He asked me if I was interested in it. I said I was. Only then did I find out about him being a witch doctor back in South Africa. Man, I tell you, from that point onwards, I just begged him to tell me as much as he could about what he did. At first, he told me to fuck off." Daniel shrugged and laughed. "I think he was suspicious of me. But after a couple of days of getting on his case, he finally told me a few things. The more he told me, the more I wanted to know. It just took me over. I dunno...it felt like he put a spell on me or something. I couldn't get enough of the shit he was doing. I looked for anything online about witch doctors. I think he liked my enthusiasm."

"So did you witness Pastor Xabi conducting any of these rituals?"

There was an uncomfortable pause; Daniel played with the skin around his fingers. His solicitor remained silent throughout the interview, on Daniel's wishes. "Yeah. I saw him kill the first boy."

Abby retrieved a picture of Michael Chauke from a brown folder and slid it across the table. "Was this the boy?"

Daniel didn't look at the picture too long. "Yeah. I drove Xabi in my van so we could dump the boy's body."

"We have a record of you purchasing a red blanket from a camping store." Scott pushed a copy of the purchase history across the table for Daniel to examine. "Can you confirm that you purchased this item?"

Daniel nodded. "Yeah, Xabi used it to wrap the boy's body."

"We have records of five children missing from the community. Two of the children have been killed. Do you know what happened to the second victim?" Scott put forward two pictures of five-year-old Nathi Buhari. Daniel's face reddened. His eyes drilled into the second picture. He appeared transfixed by the headless body.

"Daniel?"

The suspect stared up at the ceiling. "I had earned my stripes. I convinced Xabi that I was ready. He had taught me the right way to conduct what he called a muti killing. He's done tons of them back in South Africa. He taught me how to prepare, what to say, and how to do it. This little boy..." Daniel said, staring at the photograph, "was my offering to the gods. *Amandla avela empilweni entsha*," he recited. "Power comes from new life."

"And what about the other three?"

A knock on the door interrupted Abby's question. Helen poked her head in and signalled for Scott to step out. Abby confirmed for the tape recorder that the interview had been suspended and that Scott was leaving the room.

Outside, Scott folded his arms. "Not the best timing, Helen; what's up?"

"Guv, there's a gentleman in reception insisting that he needs to talk to you. Stephen, Woodman's butler."

Scott scratched his head. They had reached a crucial point in interviewing Daniel, but he needed to hear what Stephen had to say.

"Helen, you go in and tell Abby to finish off the interview. We need to find out where the other three children are and Xabi's whereabouts. I'll go and see what Stephen has to say. I don't want him kept waiting in case he has second thoughts and disappears."

45

The investigation window was fast disappearing. They had twenty-four hours left to build a case against Daniel and get it to CPS in order to charge him. The team were already working flat out, and with Mike still in hospital being checked over, he could foresee the rest of the team working through the night.

In reception, Scott greeted a frail-looking Stephen. Worry lines were etched on his forehead, and his eyes looked weary. He was a sullen, broken character.

Stephen shifted nervously on the spot as Scott shook his hand. "Stephen, thank you for coming in. Would you like to come this way?" He showed him to an open door just off the main reception.

He allowed Stephen to settle and feel comfortable in his surroundings. A member of the civilian staff came in with two cups of tea. Scott would have preferred a double espresso shot, as his body craved some wake-up juice to fight off the fatigue that was taking over.

"I...I need to tell you something, Inspector. I'm not

supposed to be here in this country. I am an illegal citizen, and I am being held here illegally."

Scott's eyes widened at the revelation. "So, let me be clear, were you brought into this country illegally, or did you make your own way here illegally?"

Stephen looked down at his tea and watched steam swirls pirouette. "I was brought here illegally as a gift for Alistair Woodman, as his private slave. But he tells everyone that I am his butler. I need your help, Inspector. I need to escape."

"We take human trafficking very seriously, Stephen. And we will do everything in our power to make sure that you're okay."

Stephen looked up and nodded, gratitude flooding his eyes as they moistened. With a trembling hand, he brought his tea to his lips. He took a few gentle sips.

"Mr Woodman is a very dangerous and angry man. He scares me. He has a lot of power and knows many people."

Scott leant forward. "Has Alistair Woodman ever been physically abusive towards you?"

Stephen paused and nodded.

"And where is Mr Woodman now?"

"He has been in London and will be arriving back soon. I need to go back before he gets home."

Scott gave a reassuring nod. "I can get a car to take you back whenever you want. However, you can choose not to go back. We can protect you."

Stephen shook his head hard. "I came here to tell you something. I hear some of his business dealings over the phone. Pastor Xabi brought me here to Mr Woodman. Pastor Xabi promised me a new life with someone rich and famous."

Stephen's information took Scott by surprise. He'd known that Stephen was troubled from the moment he met him. But Xabi's involvement was completely unexpected. This brought a whole new dimension to Scott's investigation.

He needed to know how Xabi was involved with Woodman.

46

Scott, Abby, and Helen reconvened around the incident board in the early hours of the morning. The station was quiet, nerves were frayed, and tiredness clouded their thinking. The smell of coffee wafted in the air as they gulped down their second cups, hoping the caffeine would kick in. Late-night shifts like this were not uncommon. They only had a small window of opportunity from the moment they apprehended a suspect. All officers in their situation usually forfeit a social life, sleep, and even food to ensure that everything was done by the book and in time to press charges.

Scott collapsed in a chair and ran his hands over his face. "How did the interview go?"

Abby flipped open her pad with vigour. Often, Scott thought her a machine. Sleep deprivation never seemed to bother her. Regardless of the time of day or night, she always appeared to be firing on all cylinders.

"He confirmed that Xabi murdered or, in his words, *sacrificed* the three missing children. He drove Xabi out past Falmer, where he and Xabi buried them in a pit."

Scott's buoyant mood took an instant dive as Abby relayed the details to the team. All hope of finding the children alive had been dashed. If there was one consolation, at least the families of the three children would have closure. Sometimes, the not knowing was harder to bear.

"I'm organising a couple of search-trained officers to accompany Daniel," said Scott. "He will show us the exact location of the bodies. Raj will accompany the team."

He rested his head on the back of the chair, willing himself to stay awake. "I know what the psychiatrist said, but can we be absolutely certain that Daniel Johnson is of sane mind, enough to stand trial?"

"Well, we can certainly get him assessed again," said Abby. "He's displaying psychopathic and sadistic tendencies. He sees nothing wrong in what he's done. His life is built around fantasy and fascination. When I asked him why he did what he did to the animals and the children, his reply was calm and convincing."

She checked her notes before continuing.

"He had to trap and kill animals whilst camping. He then harboured a curiosity about whether the insides of an animal looked the same as those of a human. When he met Xabi, it was the perfect opportunity to explore that."

"Nutter springs to mind," Helen commented.

Abby agreed. "When he spoke about Nathi, it was matter-of-fact. He said that the boy bled out a bit, and then he stopped. He asked me if I'd ever felt a human heart beat in my hand. And how he said it just gave me the impression that he was completely engrossed and fascinated by the whole concept. He wouldn't stop talking about how it's the body's most powerful muscle. And then he said he just wanted to see if the boys were the same on the inside."

"Inside?"

"Yes, guv. He wanted to know if black kids were the same on the inside as white kids."

Helen shook her head in consternation. "He's proper messed in the head."

A collective agreement concluded that discussion. The team reflected on Daniel's state of mind.

"And he still maintains that he's unaware of Xabi's whereabouts, Abby?" Scott asked.

"Yep. Xabi bought them a pair of pay-as-you-go phones. Not traceable. That's how he kept in touch with everyone. Daniel had to wait for Xabi's call. No one could call Xabi."

"What happened with Stephen, guv?" Helen asked. "He seemed a nervous character when he came in to see you. He wouldn't talk to me. When I said you were in an interview, he looked ready to bolt out the door again. I had to do everything I could to keep him in the station."

"You did well to keep him here."

Scott took a healthy glug of his coffee before highlighting the key points from his interview and how Woodman was in it up to his neck. Stephen explained that he knew about the gold-smuggling operation being coordinated between Pastor Xabi and Alistair Woodman. Stephen also confirmed that he knew exactly where Woodman kept all the details of the transactions.

Complicit in human trafficking, verbal and physical violence, and the illegal importation of gold. The charges were stacking up against Woodman.

"Where's Stephen now?" Helen asked.

"I've still got him downstairs. It's safer, considering the volatile situation he's in, and what he's already been subjected to. We can't afford to take a risk with his safety. My fear is that if he goes back, Woodman may already be at home, and that would be disastrous for Stephen. He's never let out of the house. He's taken a massive gamble in coming here to talk to us."

"Will he stand against Woodman?" Abby asked.

"He is happy to give us a full statement in return for his protection and the chance to return home to his family. And I think that's a good trade-off. We have someone from Woodman's inner circle who is willing to spill the beans on him. This is massive. Considering Woodman's connections with CC Lennon and other influential figures, both locally and nationally, Stephen is a vital part of this investigation and a vital witness."

Abby turned to Helen. "What's the latest on Mike?"

"He'll live. The substance that he came into contact with was neither toxic nor life-threatening. The hospital took some samples from his face and clothing for analysis. Whatever it was, it was more of an irritant and sedative. According to Raj, Mike's lips look like he'd had collagen implants, his eyes are swollen like a goldfish's, and he had a red rash on his face."

"Well, considering he's Quasimodo's half-brother, it sounds like he's better looking already." Abby chuckled. "What's our next step, guv?"

Scott stared at the incident board and narrowed in on Woodman. Doubts about Woodman had been there from the beginning. He had been itching to uncover the dirt on the man, and in the past hour, that dirt had been delivered to him on a plate.

"We go after Woodman. He's relied on Xabi to intimidate and instil fear in the families who come here. Xabi has a formidable reputation at home, and those families know it. Non-compliance on their part is met with threats to their family back home. He uses Xabi to force people to come here on the promise of a good life, in return for bringing illegal gold into this country. And Woodman is the mastermind behind it."

It could have been a story straight out of the movies. Greed, corruption, and poverty wrapped up in a heavy dose of mystical sorcery, ancient tribal beliefs, and political influence at the highest levels.

"We need to move on this. According to Stephen, Xabi came to see Woodman very late last night. I imagine it was after he disappeared from the woods. They went into the study and argued. Stephen couldn't hear what was being said. But Xabi came out not long after carrying a briefcase. It's only speculation on Stephen's part, but he presumes that whatever was in the safe was valuable. He heard Woodman say, 'Guard this with your life.'"

"Straight to Woodman's now?" Abby asked.

"Not yet. I need to wake Meadows first. Wish me luck."

47

"It's me," Woodman hissed into his phone with malice.

Xabi raised his voice. "I told you not to use this number to call me. No one is allowed to call me."

Woodman was incensed. "Listen here. When I want to talk to you, I expect you to talk to me. Don't forget it's me who's stopping your arse from going to jail. I've made you a very rich man. So cut the crap."

"*Ukuphila kwakho sekuphelile. Ukuphila kwakho sekuphelile,*" Xabi muttered.

Woodman let out a slow ripple of laughter. "Now is not the time for your mumbo-jumbo witch doctor voodoo shit."

"But it's true. Your life is over. My power has served your purpose well when it suited you. You are a foolish man to cross me. *Ukuphila kwakho sekuphelile.*"

The calm and menacing tone to Xabi's voice sent a chill through Woodman. The hairs on the back of his neck stood up.

Woodman was well aware that Xabi's reputation preceded him. He was feared wherever he went. More than two thousand pastors had been indoctrinated by him to carry out his work. His powers, his magnetism, and his reputation meant that they came from thousands of miles away to learn the ancient traditions of this craft. Businessmen, members of law enforcement the judiciary system, and fools alike would travel across his home country. They would pay huge sums to overcome physical and mental illnesses, enjoy greater wealth in business, to have misdemeanours disappear, and to seek his protection.

None of those things mattered to Woodman. He had only ever been interested in financial gain and to exert his power and influence to push his own selfish agenda. "Now is not the time to discuss the virtues of the dark arts. They are on to us. You have the goods. Take them with you."

"What are you going to do?" Xabi asked.

Woodman hung up without a reply.

He smiled to himself as he took another sip of brandy. At more than two and half grand a bottle, Louis XIII from Rémy Martin always hit the spot. The amber liquid scorched his throat and sent a wave of relaxation through his body.

"A man's home is his castle. If they think they can come and arrest me, then they are sadly mistaken." Woodman's gaze settled on the two gleaming barrels of the shotgun he had draped across his legs.

The fireplace cast long shadows over the rug in his study and dancing silhouettes on the surrounding walls. The flames curled and swayed, flicking this way and that, crackling and spitting. Brilliant flashes of yellows and whites lit up the darkened room. He walked over to the fire and watched, hypnotised, as he held out a hand to get a little more of the gentle heat one last time.

He was ready. Woodman returned to his chair, sat back, and tucked both barrels of the shotgun under his chin before closing his eyes.

48

"This'd better be good, Scott," Meadows grumbled as he walked into the incident room. His normal smart attire of a suit and shirt had been replaced with a woolly pullover, dark jeans, and worn Nike trainers. It wasn't a look that Scott and the team were used to. They took a few moments to register his change in appearance without looking too surprised.

"Sorry, sir. You know I'd only call you if it was urgent."

"Well, the missus didn't take too kindly to my phone ringing and making us both jump in bed. I would have been in the office in a few hours anyway, so this'd better be good."

Scott went through the latest updates in relation to the capture of Daniel Johnson and the involvement of Xabi and Alistair Woodman.

"And you are sure that it is a gold-smuggling operation?"

"Absolutely, sir. Xabi is bringing them into the country. They are desperate and genuine asylum seekers. They have been brainwashed into thinking that if they smuggled gold into this country, a high-ranking politician would assist their application for asylum. Xabi is such a powerful character back at home that they will believe anything he says and would do anything he asks of them."

Meadows listened; his brow furrowed in deep concentration.

"Sadly, as we know, several asylum seekers have lost their lives because of carrying gold on their persons. The children were taken first to keep the asylum seekers quiet, and to be used for the sacrificial purposes of bringing prosperity."

"Sacrificial purposes and prosperity – for what?" Meadows asked, holding out his hands.

"To bring greater wealth to the African businessmen who are coming over here to trade the gold."

"And how is Woodman implicated in all of this?"

"He's allowing the businessmen to trade the gold illegally so they can avoid paying import duties and taxes. And in return, he gets a slice of the profits. We have his butler – well, his slave. He was trafficked to the UK. He will give us a full statement."

Scott paused to give Meadows time to digest the intel that was coming in thick and fast. "And we have a ton of information now on Woodman's business dealings in South Africa. The very same businesses that he's been dealing with are the ones that are here at the moment. They are looking to exploit this legal loophole that Woodman has created for them."

"So that would explain why he's always travelling to South Africa?" Meadows glanced at the incident board.

Scott nodded. "It looks that way, sir. We need permission to get a warrant to raid Woodman's house."

Meadows paced impatiently as he weighed up his options. "Give me five minutes. I'll need the chief constable's permission. Jesus, I don't think I've ever had to call the chief in the middle of the night. I'll be back." Meadows strode off to a nearby office.

It was a nervous and anxious five minutes whilst Scott, Abby, and Helen waited for an answer. All they could do was go over the facts again, to ensure they had covered every angle, knew exactly why they needed to raid Woodman's, and what they needed to find. They were just polishing off a third round of coffees when Meadows returned.

He sighed and stretched to shake off his sleepiness. "Well, as expected, the chief constable was pissed off by my call. But I went through the facts with him. He's given us the green light. Wake up a magistrate, organise a search warrant, get the bodies together and get over there."

Excitement rippled through the officers. Abby raced to one desk, Helen to another.

"I heard Mike was injured. How is he?" Meadows asked.

"He's doing okay as far as we know, sir," said Scott. "They should be releasing him from the hospital in the next few hours. At the moment, they are keeping him in for observation."

Meadows turned to leave, but he stopped and turned back around. "You're a bit thin on the ground, so make sure you go with enough backup. And remember, Scott, this is a high-profile figure. Do everything by the book. Body cams on the second you roll through the gates. The press will be all over this one within hours of the raid. There will be a lot of interest from the government. So do this properly."

———

ONLY AN HOUR ago the blackness had been absolute. With the lightening sky and its hues reaching out to every corner and crevice, Scott and the team swept through the gates of the Oving. He'd been expecting the gates to be closed, impeding their entry, but the tactical entry team had come prepared. They had used chains to rip the gates from their housings.

The gravel drive was soon awash with job cars, several police cars, and a people carrier full of officers armed with the "big red key", an aptly named large crowbar called the "hooligan tool", bolt croppers, sledgehammer, and padlock buster.

The grim reality of the situation was in contrast to the sparrows chirping an explicit background melody to signal the arrival of a new day. Soft rays that should have brought warmth to a new day only added light to the reality of their visit.

There was a hive of activity in front of the house. Flanked on either side by uniformed officers, Scott rapped on the door several times. Other officers had made their way around to the rear of the property to look for any signs of life. After a brief pause, Scott knocked once again. When no answer was forthcoming, he gave the nod.

He keyed his radio. "Everyone in position?"

"Confirmed. Awaiting your command, guv," replied officers from the rear of the building.

Rankin, a burly uniformed officer, stood to the side of the front door. He had possession of the "big key" that would gain a fast and deafening entrance. He gave Scott the nod. "I'm good to go, guv."

Scott rested his hand on the door handle. His muscles tensed, and a bolt of adrenaline rushed through his body. He turned to look at Abby and Helen, who had the most important item, the search warrant. They both gave him a nod.

Scott looked at Rankin and then stood aside as the officer swung the fourteen-pound enforcer at the door. The door shook in its frame, unwilling to relent at first. It took Rankin three further attempts before the door submitted to the battering.

The house filled with the sound of footsteps as more than a dozen officers stepped over what remained of the front door and split off into different directions. Some raced upstairs, shouting "police" at the top of their voices. Others fanned out on the ground floor. The last person to enter the building was a uniformed officer with a large camcorder, who recorded every step of their entry and the execution of the search warrant.

A series of "clears" rang out through the property as each room was checked. As far as they understood, Woodman had returned late last night. His apparent absence surprised Scott, that was until he walked into the study.

The rear of a large wing-backed armchair faced Scott. He could see the top of Woodman's head leaning against one of the wings. The man's arms hung loosely over the sides of the armrests.

Scott walked around to the front and spotted the shotgun lying on the floor. As he looked at what remained of the lower half of Woodman's face, he shivered.

Abby placed a hand over her mouth. "That's not pretty." She walked back out again.

Helen stood shell-shocked. During her time with Scott's team, she had never witnessed the effects of a shotgun blast at close range. Fragments of bone, muscle tissue, sinews, and blood were spread across his front and the sides of the armchair.

One by one, uniformed officers came in to inspect the macabre scene.

"Helen, get forensics over here and the mortuary boys."

Better composed, Abby had returned to the room and was standing by what looked like a safe behind the desk. "Guv, over here."

Scott knelt and examined the safe. It was open and empty. "We can't be certain if this is a straightforward case of suicide or whether he died in suspicious circumstances."

"Robbery staged as a suicide? He has enough enemies," Abby speculated.

Scott shrugged. "Possibly. But he doesn't come across as the type of man who would just sit there and let someone blow off half of his face. Even if he was under duress."

49

Scott shifted through a few loose papers that lay scattered on the hearth. Official papers, bullion transaction paperwork, addresses in South Africa. He imagined that the documents were being prepared to be destroyed. Some of the paper fragments, still visible amongst the black and silvery ash, were crucial pieces of evidence. Old twisted matches and blackened wood debris also filled the still warm fireplace.

SOCOs had laid out some plastic sheeting and were picking apart the contents of the fireplace. Each fragment was photographed and documented as evidence.

Scott and Abby had wandered around Woodman's property, searching through his cupboards and drawers both upstairs and downstairs whilst the SOCOs prepared evidence downstairs. A firearms officer had made the shotgun safe, and additional forensic officers were finishing their analysis of Woodman's body.

Woodman was a collector of fine art. Pieces lined the hallway, reaching up the stairs to the first-floor landing. The collection didn't stop there. Various prints that Scott imagined dated back years were found in many of the rooms. The man certainly had expensive taste. Fine China pieces covered most surfaces. An inspection of the wardrobes in Woodman's room revealed over fifty Savile Row suits and dozens of pairs of Church's brogues.

The SOCOs gave Scott the all clear to inspect what they had retrieved from the fireplace. Scott and Abby knelt and picked through an assortment of partially burnt documents. Most had been singed brown, their edges blackened and curled.

"I have a printout here," Abby began. Her eyes narrowed as she tried to pick out a few details that were still legible. "It's showing large bank transactions to a Swiss bank. Anywhere between five and forty-five thousand pounds. It looks like he squirrelled away money."

Scott held up a piece of lined paper. "This appears to be the flight schedules for two people travelling from South Africa and the times of ferries from Dover. Thankfully, it's handwritten. I'm sure there will be a record somewhere with examples of his handwriting. We can run them through forensics for handwriting analysis. If this is Woodman's writing, then that's further proof of his involvement. These may tie in with dates and times of when people were brought in illegally."

"Well, this printout of bank transactions has the word completed written in capitals and underlined twice. That's been done by hand. So we can run that through analysis as well."

Scott's mind analysed evidence and information at a hundred miles an hour. In the space of twenty-four hours, the case had exploded and was moving at a steady rate.

"Have you found anything relating to Xabi?" Scott asked.

Abby shook her head as she continued to sift through the fragments.

All the pieces were snapping together in Scott's mind. "So, let me spell this out. Here is my theory. Woodman was taking backhanders to ensure that the gold dealers could trade their gold on the black market in the UK without detection. The undervalued goods were sold with high profit margins. Woodman was given his share."

"Sounds about right," Abby said, nodding.

"He developed his contacts from his various visits to South Africa and set up the deals at their end. When the bullion dealers came here, their business was shielded by Woodman. He colluded with Xabi to use asylum seekers as mules to bring gold into this country, and he relied on Xabi to keep the mules quiet. He was the go-between."

Scott picked up another piece of paper, which had what appeared to be the remains of partial index numbers. Only one index number appeared to be intact. When Scott did a PNC check on it, it came back as a white Mercedes Sprinter van. He waved the sheet of paper at Abby.

"With this type of van, it's not too difficult to put in a false floor or false walls to hide illegals. The vans came in through Dover. Mules were promised a better life with the backing of the local MP. Xabi not only arranged for the illegals to be brought in, but also collected the gold from the poor bastards."

Abby continued his train of thought. "Which meant the bullion dealers could come and go without having to carry any of the gold. Clever."

Scott agreed. "Exactly. And with gold fetching more than a thousand pounds per ounce at the moment, it's a lucrative business. Two years ago, it was running at around eight hundred and fifty pounds per ounce. Big risks, high return."

"No wonder Woodman was keen to support the Home Office's decision to deport the asylum seekers. He wanted to get rid of the evidence. They were his weak link, and Stephen's proven that."

"Abby, contact all the airports and ports across the southeast. We need them to be on the lookout for Xabi. Supply them with his picture, his description, and the reasons we need to detain him. I can't believe that despite all our efforts, we haven't found the slippery git."

"Maybe he's magicked himself away," Abby replied, making a ghostly woo noise.

"Magic, my arse," Scott fired back. "He's a murderer, plain and simple. He gets off on instilling fear in people, and he's done so for many years. People back home believe he really does have some type of magical power. We need to find him. That's our priority. Get Helen to help you and lean on Pastor Joshua Mabunda. He must know more about Xabi's movements. Mabunda's still in the frame for something. Not sure what yet."

50

X abi made his way through the passenger terminal. Hordes of travellers rushed in all directions, excited about their forthcoming trips to the continent. Parents dragged children from one desk to another. The distant sound of a child crying echoed through the large building. A crescendo of spoken conversations added to the ambient sounds.

He could see the passengers' curiosity about him. They nudged each other as he walked through. To many, he might resemble the black version of Freddy Krueger. Frightened children gripped their parents' legs as he passed them. He represented the real face of Halloween up close and personal. Parents did their hardest to divert their children's eyes from him, on his way to the entry point for the ferry.

The sound of cars rolling up the ramp and into the bowels of the ship reached him from below. The slight rumble of the various engine and air-conditioning systems signalled the ferry would soon depart.

He was next in line to be seen by the passenger service assistant at the doors to the ferry. He waited in line before stepping up to take his turn. The assistant smiled, but perhaps for a second too long. She glanced nervously at the ticket Xabi thrust at her.

The assistant went through the details, then smiled uneasily. He knew it was a false smile, but he smiled back anyway.

"Welcome aboard, Pastor Xabi, for your journey from Dover to Calais. I hope you have a safe and pleasant trip." She waved him through.

Within ten minutes, the ferry had inched away from the White Cliffs of Dover. He stared through the window at the green-topped cliffs and the hive of activity beneath. Within ninety minutes, he would step onto French soil. From there, he would head south towards Spain, following the coast to Almeria before crossing over to Algeria. He had planned to cross eastward across the African continent, passing through Congo, Tanzania, and Malawi before heading south to South Africa. He had planned his route carefully to avoid many of the well-trodden routes African migrants followed when chasing a better life in Europe.

Back home, he could resume his work, knowing that no one would come looking for him.

ABBY CAME RUSHING BACK to Scott. "He's slipped the net, guv. He boarded a ferry at Dover about thirty minutes ago."

Scott shook his head in disbelief and slumped back against his car. The possibility of detaining Xabi appeared to be slipping through his fingers. His mind raced as he considered all options left. He pulled up Google on his phone and looked into ferry timetables.

He shot Abby a glance. "It's a ninety-minute journey. Get the port authorities to inform security on the ferry that we're searching for him. Then contact the French authorities. They can pick him up the minute he steps off."

"Will do, guv." Abby bolted back indoors.

He shouted in her wake, "And tell them we want confirmation the minute they pick him up. We're bringing that bastard back to Dover."

SCOTT PACED NERVOUSLY around Abby's desk, to the extent that she ordered him to sit down.

Security personnel on the ship confirmed with port authorities that they had located Xabi but had not approached him. That news encouraged Scott. A mixture of elation and anxiety coursed through his body. He couldn't rest until he had that phone call.

A little over an hour later, Abby's phone rang to confirm that Pastor Xabi had been detained and arrested on suspicion of murder. Scott squeezed Abby's shoulder in recognition of her hard work and their result.

THE JOURNEY TIME took them a little over two hours. For most of the journey, they remained silent. Scott drove along the coast road while Abby looked out to sea, lost in her thoughts.

Occasionally, they spoke about the case, but their thoughts were too consumed with the trail of destruction that had been left by one man and a greedy politician. They had affected and taken so many lives. Young children who hadn't experienced the world had had their lives extinguished in the most brutal and sadistic of ways.

The repercussions of this case would be felt for years in political circles and amongst the local community. The media storm that would follow would soon swallow up the real victims and their continuing plight. That saddened Scott.

XABI SAT HANDCUFFED in an interview suite with Dover police, showing no emotion. Scott itched to grab him and throw him across the room. He'd expected remorse. Maybe even regret at his capture. Anger. Instead, his expression remained flat.

He stared ahead as Scott and Abby faced him. Having spent almost two weeks on this case, it felt like a bittersweet moment for Scott. He had the main perpetrator in front of him, but the man showed no signs of guilt. Xabi chose instead to speak in his preferred language, muttering things that neither officer nor their French counterparts could understand.

The words that Scott thought he'd never get the opportunity to say slipped from his mouth.

"Pastor Xabi, I'm arresting you on suspicion of the abduction and murder of Michael Chauke. I'm also arresting you on suspicion of assisting unlawful immigration under Section 25 and facilitating entry by asylum seekers to the UK for gain under Section 25A of the Immigration Act." He thought of Stephen as he delivered his final statement. "I'm also arresting you on suspicion of arranging to facilitate travel of another person with a view to exploitation, under the Modern Slavery Act 2015."

WE HOPE YOU ENJOYED THIS BOOK

If you could spend a moment to write an honest review on Amazon, no matter how short, we would be extremely grateful. They really do help readers discover new authors.

ALSO BY JAY NADAL

Printed in Great Britain
by Amazon

21782795R00169